'The language is cons

something I have not yet ⌞⌞⌞⌞ ⌞⌞ ⌞ur literature – the meld of Scottish and northern Irish. It's both a chasm and a bridge. Fascinating stuff. And Donal obviously knows it very well.

'I really like the characters – their vibrancy, their obsessions. And the great strength of these pieces – when stepped away from for a while – is their collective impact. I feel like I have stepped into a secret, although I'm not entirely sure what secrets I should or should not know.'

Colum McCann

A young boy, new to Scotland, is attacked by older pupils from the local secondary school as he plays with sticks in a puddle. The same boy – Liam – mistakes the Mona Lisa for the Virgin Mary and prays to avoid being belted. When God Save the Queen is played, he races his brothers and sisters to be the one to switch the TV off. On rare returns to Derry, he witnesses the Troubles from his gran's livingroom. Goodbyes can't be said quickly enough at the end of a first such holiday. Soldiers turn up during another – to raid the house. The boy hears stories on these occasions too. A cousin is offended by a course book at school. A hypnotist performs across the border – with tragi-comic consequences. In the final Liam story in this collection, the O'Donnells have visitors from Derry as Jim Watt fights Charlie Nash for a world championship title.

Throughout the book, these Irish-Scottish stories from a 1970s childhood and youth alternate with stories with more recent and/ or international settings. A father and son drive to East Germany a month after the Wall comes down. A German school-leaver travels alone, north of Inverness. A reticent father spends time alone in his adult son's new flat. Two friends, returning from holiday, discuss one's broken relationship. A successful salesman, on business in Austria, hears the tale of a Viennese counterpart. An elderly couple, on holiday on Lanzarote, are not content with the 'package'. A lapsed Catholic may (or may not) return to Confession as the Vatican announces a Holy Year.

McLaughlin takes his lead from Alfred Andersch, whose Franz Kien stories – a loose sequence, to which each new collection added – reflect life in the Weimar Republic and Third Reich. 'Deutscher Architekt', as they say. Throw in McLaughlin's passion for Scottish and Irish writing of the past thirty years, and the result is captivating.

an ALLERGIC REACTION to NATIONAL *anthems*

and other stories

Donal McLaughlin

ARGYLL ✤ PUBLISHING

First published in 2009 by
Argyll Publishing
Glendaruel
Argyll PA22 3AE
Scotland
www.argyllpublishing.com

The author has asserted his moral rights.

**British Library Cataloguing-in-Publication Data.
A catalogue record for this book is available from
the British Library.**

ISBN 978 1 906134 39 6

Printing: Bell & Bain Ltd, Glasgow

For my family

in Scotland
in Ireland
& elsewhere

first & foremost:
my mother
& father

for friends
I regard as family

and for
Liam's godmother
as it were
— Stella

Contents

They were living at the top of the 59 Steps at the time, and outside their door the street veered away to the right, round to the shops wi the CO-OP at one end and GALBRAITHS at the other, one was light-blue, Liam remembers, the other bright red: he could've done wi an explanation for that at the time.

Anyway: one day he was playing at the gutter on the curve, diagonally opposite the house, wi his brother, Sean, or some other youngfella – he doesn't mind. He does know he was still at Primary at the time cos he was wearing the red, black and white tie, and him and the other youngfella were totally lost in the puddles and ice-pop sticks and stuff, watching rainbow colours forming patterns on the surface of the water.

It's possible the other youngfella deliberately sank some of their 'boats' and that Liam had to tell him to *currit out*, maybe even to *currit, right?* Or then again, maybe they were being *best muckers*. What *is* sure is that anyone passing would've realised the weeboys at the gutter – or Liam, at least – was Irish and Catholic.

And that's what happened: a guy from the Secondary on the far side of the playing fields at the other end of the estate passed wi his mate, both wearing the blue and gold ties of their school, and he'd actually gone past when he stopped and turned back and got hold of Liam's tie, and as he lifted him, he said something Liam didn't catch cos a knee made contact wi his balls, not that he'd've known to call them that yet, or *testicles* either, sure they'd hardly descended, even, and knowing Liam and his upbringing, he wouldn't've known to expect them to.

What Liam does mind, apart from standing there, not knowing what to do and not knowing what to say, is: sort-of panicking in his head, his brain jamming, thinking *Didn't know about this – Nobody told me about this*, while down-below – which seemed a long way away – was signalling he was maybe going to faint.

The two guys from the Secondary left it at that and walked away, assuring each other it was the right thing to do, no more than these Paddies deserved. *Why don't they stay in their own fuckin country,* that's what their dads said.

There wasn't a boo out of Sean, or whoever the other youngfella was, during all of this. He just looked sorry for Liam, or guilty, and returned to their 'boats'. When Liam finally got down on his hunkers but and gradually started playing again, the other weeboy gave him the best 'boat' and said, 'Here – *you* take that!'

aka La Giaconda 2

for Christoph & Birgit

The smell of bubblegum and 'Liam – '

That was how it started: a penny-bubbly smell and Tait sounding nice for once.

'*Liam* – '

'What?'

It was out before he knew it. There he'd been: careful, one minute – on his guard, lik – wondering what the trap was this time? Then it goes and slips out and thon sneaky snidey smile of Tait's starts to cross the shit-hawk's face and sure enough: 'Liam O'Donnell – OUT!' La Giaconda's roaring. 'I SAW YOU! Don't even think of denying it! Out to the front for talking!' and he's caught, – *conned,* been tricked into talking, and while he's busy disentangling himself from school-bags and *CELTIC* bags, even the odd *ST MIRREN* bag, she's giving it: 'OUT! I SAID! Out to the front and face the wall!' and just to rub it in, he has to squeeze past Tait and his smirk and he'd love to knock the smile off that bugger's face, he can't but, not now, so he concentrates on getting to the wall before – AND YOU CAN JUST WAIT THERE, BOY, UNTIL I'M READY TO DEAL WITH YOU!

O Jesus. O sweet Jesus. He was in for it now, okay. And themmins all watching an' all. He didn't need eyes in the back of his head to know that. He could just see them rubbing their hands at the thought of it: thought of *that effin wee paddy*, caught, finally landed in it. Could see McGoldrick, Bawjaws & Co watching your woman laying into him. The girls were different: they'd be working away, part from stopping to flick away their fringes. Only a cheeky eagle-eyed bitch lik Margaret-Mary might be on the look-out for ammo. Thon time Bobo got belted, was her spotted the skitters –

He was in for a long wait: Miss was checking their New Decimals still. Least – back in Derry – he'd've had to go and pick his stick. At Faughanvale, the teacher sent ye out to the hawthorn bush and if there wasn't enough thorns on the stick ye brought back, ye got taken by the ear and shown how to choose a proper one. Here was worse but: even just the *look* of the belt, fact it had two fingers. Also the way ye had to hold your hands: the one not getting hit holding up the one that was. O Jesus. His mickey was sore just thinking bout it.

'DEREK O'NEILL!'

Liam jumped even though it wasn't him even.

'What's *this*?? 7-1??'

'A Celtic-Rangers score, Miss – '

'A football score? A football score *in my classroom*??' La Giaconda roared.

She wasn't half on the war-path today, Christ! Liam could just imagine her – the jotter held up in disgust.

'I'm sorry, Miss!' Derek said.

'*I'm sorry, Miss*,' she mimicked. 'I'll *sorry-Miss* you, boy! I want a fresh cover on that jotter by tomorrow!'

There was a pause, for one of them sarcky wee smiles of hers, then *Thank God!* he heard her walking away. Liam felt the relief go through him. If more than one ended up out, they'd *all* get belted – that was for sure. This way, if he was lucky –

He stopped himself. *Coward's thinking*, that's what that was.

He told himself to think of something else. To be a man, naw a sparrow.

aka aka aka. They'd been like a bunch of wee parrots wi their bloody *aka-s*. Least it was in the dictionary, unlike *Giaconda* –

Giaconda: they'd him thinking that now an' all – even though he didn't know the reason. It had all started when he was off, helping Mum have wee Orla. Miss must've said it one day, and themmins picked up on it. They'd other new sayings an' all. They kept getting Lazarus, for instance, to say *the human insistence on comprehending*. Cos of his lisp maybe. Also: any time they got Painting now, they showed off wi their palettes and put on voices to praise the *microscopically tiny brush strokes*. Their favourite word was subtlety.

Liam just hoped he wouldn't be found out: not knowing, not understanding. He got enough slaggins as it was.

Uh-oh, a high-heel alert: Miss was coming to the front.

If she went to the second drawer on the right, he was *dead*.

He braced himself. That's what his Granda Cluskey always did: *braced himself*.

Christ, she *was*: She was heading for the desk. Liam could just imagine Tait's face, the *satisfaction*. It was OK but: she wasn't sitting down. Usually, she sat down to dig for the belt and the discipline book. She always wrote down how many and what for fore she gave ye them. *Masochist*. Sometimes her shoe slipped off and she had to put it on again first.

Nup, he was OK. It was her mouth she was goney open. Not her desk.

'Your undivided attention, Primary 7!'

He heard their pencils going down, people sitting up straight.

'We'll be doing Art after the interval,' Giaconda announced. 'While you finish your Arithmetic, therefore, I shall fetch the Leonardo in the Medical Room. I warn you, however: there'll be no Art if a single individual utters one word while I'm out. *Understood?*'

'Yes, Miss.'

'Good! Remember that! O'Donnell, you take the names of any talkers!'

The click of her heels had hardly faded fore they started:

> *'Liam!'*
>
> 'What?'
>
> *'Out for talking!'*
>
>> *'Liam!'*
>>
>> 'What?'
>>
>> 'Out for talking!'

The chorus was growing.

Liam ignored them. *Sticks and stones*, that's what the librarian had said. *Sticks and stones can break my bones, but words, they cannot hurt me.*

'Hope ye're taking the names o' talkers, Paddy!' someone sneered. Everyone laughed. It sounded lik Ironside, wi his calliper and gammy leg.

It wasn't true: words could so hurt.

A hush, all of a sudden. They must've realised Curran would be across the landing if they didn't watch and then Giaconda would be really raging.

Liam felt their looks boring into him. No matter how he tried, he couldn't work out why they done this. Wasn't cos he was a Catholic. They were too, sure.

He was just after stiffening his legs, determined not to look scared, at least, when a paper aeroplane nearly took his cheek off. It crashed against the wall and fell to the floor. He looked down. There was writing on the wings. FILLING YOUR NAPPY R U? it said on one. WAY HOME TO FUCKINVALE PADDY, on the other.

Shit-hawks! he thought. He *wanted* to understand them, couldn't but. Just couldn't fathom them at all. They were an *enigma*. All their wee digs.

Maybe his da was right: maybe that was the way Scots were. His da didn't lik them.

O Jesus. If his da didn't lik them either –

Jesusjesusjesus.

He sneaked a look over his shoulder: the classroom crucifix.

God-o-god-o-god.

Maybe he should *pray*!

St Harry of Houdini!

Folk always laughed, his Uncle Seamus swore by him but –

UH-OH another high-heel alert: Miss was on her way back up.

Least there was no talking. For once, no-one was talking –

Then he remembered the plane.

O Holy God. On a hiding to nothing, he was. If he bent down and picked it up, themmins would give him hell. If he didn't, Giaconda would. She'd blow her buckin top!

Her footsteps were getting closer and closer when *Chicken!* he lowered himself to snatch the bloody thing up.

'Well, O'Donnell, did anyone talk?' Miss asked as she struggled wi the door, her arms full of white paper and paint-brushes and paint-pots.

'No, Miss. No-one,' he replied as *ultra*-carefully she put down a tiny wee picture-frame.

He'd hardly answered, half-expecting God to strike him dead, when the door flew open again. Liam froze. It could only be –

Sure enough: the class was jumping to its feet.

'Good morn-ing, Mr Cud-di-hy!' they chorused. From the sounds of them, Liam wasn't the only one afraid Cuddihy knew they'd been talking.

'Mornin!' the headmaster answered, not one bit friendly. Liam thought back to the Faughanvale principal –

'Liam O'DONNELL!!'

Liam froze again.

'What are *you* doing out?'

Buck, he thought. This was getting worser. Now Cuddihy would belt him: Cuddihy, who'd a reputation for being *vicious*. He turned to face him. Head hadn't waited for an answer but. He'd turned to the teacher instead.

'What's *he* doing out?'

Giaconda looked affronted. The Head was telling her off, for some reason. She tried to whisper, to wave Cuddihy round the back of the blackboard. Liam's heart sank – even moreso when Cuddihy re-emerged, snapped, 'Mornin, you lot!' and left. Miss would make his life misery now, alright.

He could hear the deep breaths she was taking.

Next thing he knew, she was making a beeline for him.

'Close your eyes, boy!'

She'd been *smoking* – he could smell it.

'EYES CLOSED, I SAID!'

He closed them, half-expecting a thump. She was hovering beside him.

'Describe the wall in front of you!' she demanded.

'What now?' he asked.

In Derry, ye sometimes got *three pages on the inside of a pingpong ball by tomorrow.*

'What now?' she mimicked. 'Of course, NOW!'

Liam couldn't begin to start. He'd rather've been given the composition. Even the hard version: *avoiding the words* ping *and* pong.

'Well?'

All he could mind were cracks, flakes, a dirty yellow colour. Ye couldn't get a sentence out of that. And knowing Giaconda, she'd want a whole paragraph: light and shade etc. He remembered the silhouettes. That there was a Mr Silhouette. *Had been*, in seventeenth-century France.

'The wall is a discoloured yellow colour – ' he began.

'Repetition of *colour*!' she warned.

'And silhouettes are on display – '

'Too vague!' she complained. 'How many?'

'Doh-no,' he mumbled.

'Pardon?'

'I don't know, Miss.'

'Well, we'll just have to let you stand here longer then, won't we?'

He opened his eyes. Another wee sarcky smile for his collection. He gulped, then spotted a nail he could've mentioned. A nail wi nothing on it.

The door squeaked open again.

Jesus, it was Cuddihy, back! Wi his strap, maybe.

'Good morn-ing, Fa-ther Kielt!'

It was only the priest, thank God. Hah! Served them right. Now they'd be getting their catechism, instead of Painting. Better still: Giaconda would have to send him back to his seat. She wouldn't belt him in front of the priest.

It was a *miracle* –

Or maybe it wasn't: way they were buckin talking, Father wouldn't be staying.

Sure enough, soon they were agreeing he'd visit the following week. That would suit *Lisa* (as he called her) *perfectly*. The children would prepare something for him. And yes, she'd *love* to do the flowers for the altar.

Father was heading to the door.

'Say goodbye to Fr Kielt, boys and girls!' Giaconda said. *Lik butter wouldn't melt.*

'Good-bye, Fa-ther Kielt!'

'Goodbye, children, and God bless!'

Just as it seemed lik he'd gone, he spoke again.

'Be seeing you at Confession on Saturday night then, shall I?'

It was him! The priest was talking to him!

'Turn round when Father's speaking to you, child!' Giaconda said.

Liam turned. Priest was preparing to lay hands on him.

'Just see if I can do my *Exorcist* bit, shall I?' he said to the teacher and winked.

Giaconda actually *smiled*.

Priest put his hand on Liam's forehead and whispered things in Latin. The hand was all sweaty and his breath smelt of Christ's blood. Liam felt the most amazing holiness rush through him. He was so nervous, he nearly wet himself. Managed to stop his mickey just in time but.

'That's better!' Father announced when he was done. 'You'll have no more bother wi this boy now, Mrs McMenemy!'

He turned to Liam. 'Still want to see you at Confession on Saturday night, though, youngfella!'

'Yes, Father!'

'Promise?'

'Promise.'

'Tell your daddy to toddle along an' all! It won't do him any harm.'

Ye'd've thought the Virgin Mary, if she was goney show, would've turned up while the priest was there. She waited until he'd left but. Liam nearly choked when he turned to face the wall again and saw her – *sweet Mother of God!* – where the nail had been.

Buckin rotters! When he'd asked what he'd missed in Art, they'd laughed and talked in riddles. Smart-ass stuff about *A Picture of a Famous Woman*. Or *A Famous Picture of a Woman*. They'd said both, switching the word 'famous' lik them boys on *Going for a Song*. Not a single mention of the Blessed Virgin but. Shit-hawks! All they had to say was: it was a painting of Our Lady. Did they but? Did they buck!

Miss hadn't told him what he'd missed either.

It wasn't the Virgin he was used to. Was more lik his mammy's Child of Prague. Or lik the icon, up in the loft. Strange thing was: she was wearing *brown*, for some reason.

Liam decided to pray to her anyhow, shuffled along to be more in front of her. He joined his hands. *Hail Mary, full of Grace*, he began, trying his best to be holy. He was goney try his *damnedest*, realised just in time but: Mary could think he was cursing.

– *Please*, Mary, let me not be belted.

– *Holy Mary, Mother of God*, make her let me off.

– I'll be good.

– I promise.

He started a Rosary without meaning to.

At the end of the first decade, he looked to see was it working. Was it hell! Was as if she was sniggering. As if she was totally unimpressed. He couldn't believe the Blessed Virgin could be lik that.

He'd have to pray harder. What he needed was the special, holy-holy prayers his mammy and granny knew. *Hail Holy Queen, Mother of Mercy* would do the trick: *hail our life, our sweetness and our hope*. Thon kinda stuff!

He tried to look her in the eye, despite the funny look she was giving him. *Im-plore* her, that's what his granny would say. He could just see them all, down on their knees up in the Creggan, *mourning and weeping this valley of tears*. Rhyming it off, they'd be: *To thee do we cry, to thee do we send up our sighs*. Their Derry accents –

He stared at Mary and concentrated, *concentrated*, thinking: im-plore, im-plore, I *im-plore* ye.

It was no use. Nothing was happening. She hadn't even joined her hands even!

Wasn't as if she was nursing the Baby Jesus, either!

Naw, her left hand was holding her right wrist just.

It was all puffy, Liam noticed.

She was a funny-looking colour an' all, now he looked at her. Not kind and beautiful lik in other pictures. Heaven was all-horrible, into the bargain. Protestant must've painted it.

This was what he got for not wearing his medals. Not carrying his rosary beads.

He wanted his mammy, knew she'd be busy making stews but.

He knew what she'd say, anyhow. Didn't need three guesses. 'Mind, now!' she'd say. 'And always say your prayers! For the Good Lord works in mysterious ways!'

He'd no choice but to give it one last go.

Stand up straight, he thought. And be all-holy. Lik when Fr Kielt blissed ye.

I'll *never* sin *ever* again, he vowed.

He only succeeded in deciding Giaconda to belt him but.

He did – he decided her – he *must've* – cos she was heading for the desk.

This was definitely it.

It *was*.

It was lik her eyes were fixed on him, lik she wanted to watch him *suffer*.

Close your eyes, stupid, and *pray*, he tried to tell himself. His imagination was running away wi him but.

He magined her opening the drawer and his mickey stirred.

He magined her slowly taking the belt out. Aw naw, he was goney pee!

'Hands out!' she would say – his mickey shifted again – and if he held out only one, she'd insist on the other one, too.

AAW NNAAAWWW!!

His mickey was going thon sore kinda way.

Turn then, most gracious advocate, he prayed quickly, *thine eyes of mercy towards us*

RIGHT AWAY, PLEASE!!

Mary was now *levitating* beside him. Must've clambered out of the picture-frame somehow.

Her perfume was lovely.

He could feel her hovering there, giving him strength – not that he dared to look.

He reached out to take her hand. It was more lik she took his but and raised it up. It felt that holy. Then she took his other one but – to make it support the first.

Aw Jesus *nnaaaww*: her and Giaconda were ganging up!

He was nearly pulling away when he realised this was a *test*. Surely she wouldn't abandon him in his hour of need? Surely she would be there *at his last agony*? Sure enough: soon, her hands were beneath his, holding them in position. They were shoulder-to-shoulder now, practically. Him and the Virgin Mary: shoulder-to-shoulder, four hands as one.

It felt nice. Soft. Lik one of his mammy's cuddles nearly.

Even without opening their eyes, their eyes met.

O clement, o loving, o sweet Virgin Mary, he bubbled.

She smiled, *beatifically*.

'Be not afraid, child!' she whispered – so as not to get caught. 'When her there lets fly, I'll place my hand, the hand *of the Mother of God*,' she intoned, 'over yours.'

'What if it stings but?' he blurted.

'Sh-sh-sh,' she warned.

'There will be no sting, child,' she promised.

The bell went for playtime. Liam didn't jump so much as nearly shit himself. When he saw where his hands were, he pulled them down again, sharpish. Blessed Virgin, thank God, had got her arse back into the picture *pronto*.

Liam looked to check: *Phew* –

Themmins hadn't spotted nothing. Or – for once – weren't saying nothing.

They traipsed past without the usual rush for the tuckshop.

'You're dead!' Tait signalled when he passed.

Mary smiled at him again – same smile, different but – once they'd gone.

Finally, there was nothing but the terrible click of Giaconda's heels. She was coming up behind him. He heard her alright. Smelt her an' all. Still jumped a bit but when her hand landed on his shoulder.

'On you go, O'Donnell!' she said. 'Skedaddle!'

Liam didn't wait for a gold invitation. For her to hiss to get out of her sight.

He legged it.

'Oh – and O'Donnell – ' she called after him.

Aw naw! Stupid shite: he was running in the corridor!

That's not what she said but.

'Leave Tait to me!' she warned – and smiled.

the old block 3

To let you see it from my point-of-view: it's Friday night, I've just put my feet up before going out, when – totally out of the blue – the phone goes, and without so much as a 'Hello' or 'How are ye?' she's deafening my right ear nearly:

LISTEN TO THIS, YOU

LISTEN TO THIS, PADDY McEVOY

TO WHAT I HAVE TO BUCKIN WELL PUT UP WI

Not a cheep comes down the line, of course. I can just see her but: over at the wee table, up in Aberdeen, holding the receiver up to let me hear the racket. And I'm wondering who the culprit is this time when

OH AYE!

comes down the line

TYPICAL!

WELL SEEN THEY'RE ALL QUIET NOW ALRIGHT

TEARING THE HAIR OUT OF EACH OTHER A MINUTE AGO THEY WERE!

'Who?' I ask, despite myself. 'Seamus an' that wee shite Dominic,' says she, and part of me's thinking: here we go again! Is thinking: I came down to London to *get away from* this. I don't say nothing but. I think the better of it. I feel myself giving up just, giving in again. All that comes out is a 'Chrissake, woman!' That riles her even more, of course:

DON'T YOU BUCKIN 'WOMAN' ME!

she roars

I DON'T HAVE TO TAKE THAT FROM YOU

I DON'T HAVE TO TAKE THAT FROM ANYBUCKINONE

WHAT I WANT TO KNOW'S WHEN YOU'RE GOIN TO START TAKING A BUCKIN INTEREST IN THIS HERE YOUNGFELLA?

And I know from that it's Dominic's in the doghouse, she's got it in for the youngfella, has had from Day One, and I'm imagining the look on the weeboy's face – and fizzing at the thought of that other big lump – when she comes away wi a cracker, a total fuckin classic:

HERE! – YOUR FATHER SAYS TO PUT YOU ON!

I hadn't said a word, of course.

There's a silence as the youngfella comes to the phone, and I can just see the triumphant look on her face, this is worse than wait-till-your-father-gets-home, this is, and as I wait for him, it occurs to me I don't know what he's thinkin. He could be afraid I'll come on heavy, I realise, and I'm wondering whether to tell him his mother's at it – when I hear her giving it, 'Get a move on, would ye?' and then a wee voice says

Hel-lo ?

not a big round, it's-great-to-hear-from-you HELLO, but

Hel-lo ?

and you know to listen to him he's scared shitless, that he doesn't know what might hit him next

and it breaks your heart and that's why I say

'Yes, mucker!' like I'm putting my arm round him
and I wait for him to hear that, till I think he can sense I'm not
about to tear strips off him, then I say

'Look, son – ' and again the *son* is nice as anything

'Look, son, you don't have to say anything. Just answer me Yes
or No.'

'Is it bad?'
and I can hear the change in him as his guard begins to drop, then
he says

'Aye, Da – '
in a way that goes through me – and that's it, there's only one
thing for it:

'D'you want to come down an' visit?' I ask, thinking of all the
reasons not to, trying not to let them into my voice but, and – God
love him – he says

'Aye, Da'
like I'd offered him an ice-cream and that goes through me too:
him starting to hope, him that came to the phone scared now
thinking his coupon's up, so I forget any reservations I had and say

'Right, tell that mother o yours to put you on the Nightrider.
You'll still make it.'

'Tell her I'll pay for you at this end if I have to – '

He must've covered the receiver for some reason cos I didn't
hear him. Next thing I know, his mother's back and I say

'I take it that's all right with you then?'

I put it that way deliberately – defying her to say no.

'You can do whatever you buckin like – as long as I get my

money back' says she. I can tell she's surprised but, that I've caught her on the hop –

'Course you'll get your money,' says I, 'I'll send it up in an envelope.'

'Bout buckin time you did your share!' says she and slams the phone down.

Course, no sooner do I put the phone down than it rings again – me that never gets any calls! – and I'm about to hiss

'Phoned to apologise, have you?'

when I hear it's Barry from the office and he's asking me to take a lorryload over to Germany in the morning. Jesus, Mary and Joseph, I think to myself: thinking of our Dominic on his way down – even if he wouldn't't've left the house yet. I could call and postpone it, of course, but the weeboy's upset enough as it is, so I take a deep breath and make sure Barry suspects nothing cos the way things are down here, you have to seem keen.

'Course I'll do it!' I announce.

'Knew I could count on you, squire! Be here for nine,' he says, then claims he has to go. That the other phone's ringing.

I was at King's Cross for half six, I was so bloody determined the youngfella wouldn't get off the train to discover I wasn't there. Thought of him alone on the platform sent shivers through me. Youngfella's been through enough. His big brothers and sisters got a better deal – least in the days when Eileen and I could still look at each other. I saw the world of difference in him when he stepped off the train.

'Fit like, Da?' says he. He can be that broad at times – our only Aberdonian. The only one not born in Ireland.

'Yes, mucker!' says I. 'How's the form?' – and I look him in the eye and give him a hug to match the smile. 'How's everyone?' and he starts telling me and I listen – and let him see I'm listening. I'm not saying much myself, I'm enjoying the craic but – though it hurts when he puts me in mind of my weegirls. Rosie, especially.

We get so carried away, I nearly forget to tell him about Barry – I'm so busy watching him.

He's a wee natural. And talking to me like we were never apart.

There's no mention of his mother or Seamus. He'll tell me in his own time, maybe.

We're still walking and talking, without me saying nothing, when, finally, I have to interrupt him. 'I'm not interrupting you or anything, son,' I say, 'but there's something I have to tell you – '

His wee face changes.

'There's a bit of a problem, son – '

Ye want to've seen the alarm across his face.

'I got another phone call, mucker. I've to set off in an hour wi a lorry-load.'

'And what about me, like?' he blurts out. 'I'm not going straight back up, if that's what you're thinking!'

'Christ, naw, son – that's not what I'm thinking,' I say, thinking:

FOOL!

'Naw, son, you're not going back. I wouldn't be here to put you on the train, for starters. Naw, you're coming wi me. To Germany.'

His wee face lights up.

'Germany?'

'Aye, Germany.'

He doesn't even ask what his mother'll think.

Give Barry his due: truck was ready and loaded when we got there and he handed over the paperwork. I was glad of that: didn't want Dominic at the gate too long, even if he could see me. Didn't want Barry knowing the youngfella was there either, of course. Which is why I done everything I normally would – took time to walk round the truck, checking it was all securely tied etc. Then it was up and in as if I was setting off, even though I'd be pulling in just beyond the gate.

That's when it hit me: the porn –

Jesus fuck: there was tits and fannies everywhere. Fuckin hell, I thought. I realised too but I couldn't take them down. Barry would see me. Or some other boy in the office. I'd never live it down. Fuck it, I thought and did a quick shuffle, hiding the worst of them.

Dominic clocks them, of course. Soon as he jumps in. Be more worried if he didn't, I suppose.

He sits there, proud as punch, patting the leather seat.

'So what d'ye think?' I ask.

'Aye, naw bad!' he answers.

Then he comes away wi an absolute cracker. 'Nice photies!' says he. 'Did ye take them yourself?'

I pretend to knock his pan in and we gut ourselves. He's not finished but: 'That one there could be Mrs Breslin!' says he, and that does it – two of us are *helpless*. Pissin ourselves, we are, at the thought of the Blessed bloody Mary going topless.

'Your mother would kill me!' I manage to splutter when I stop choking.

'It's alright! I won't tell – ' says he.

I chuck him a Raisin an' Biscuit Yorkie.

'Here, shove that down ye. Keep ye goin!'

We get to the boat in plenty of time.

I show him a few manoueuvres. He watches, well impressed. I trot out my usual 'Give me the space between the wall and the wallpaper, an' I'll park anything!' He laughs. Likes the idea. 'I'll teach you when you're old enough!' I say. He nods. Dead keen.

The boat's a winner too. Fact it's got a cinema. Even if he's seen the pictures they're showing. Fair play to the other lads an' all: when we join them in the cafe, they treat him like one of their own. He has me feeling right proud: he's not one bit shy, has a bit o craic to offer – and laps it up when the other guys warm to him. I have to think back to what he was like in the house. What he would've been like last night even.

By the time we go on deck I realise what a lucky bugger I am. He could hate me, Dominic. Could refuse to have anything to do wi me. And here we are: and it feels like he hasn't a thing against me.

He cuddles in to me when it gets too cold for him.

Feels like no time before we're rolling off again. 'Welcome to Holland!' says I. And he's looking at – *everything*, trying to guess what the billboards are all about – and he's doing rightly, far as I can tell myself. When I stop at the first Services, he pretends to kiss the ground: just about prostrate, he is, till I say – *Aw right, John Paul, ye can get up now!* He laughs and makes a beeline for the shop. Soon, he's listening to the folk in front of him, hoping to hear Dutch. He makes out he's learned some. '*Raider* is Dutch for *Twix*, Da!' he tells me. 'And *Snickers* is a *Marathon*!'

I had to laugh.

'Just one local pick-up, mucker, and we'll be on our way proper!' I tell him.

We end up getting messed about but. All over empty cable-reels. So much for it being URGENT.

When we did get moving, it wasn't long before his eyes were closing. I knew the feeling and pulled over at a service area. He woke when I tried to put a cover over him.

'You're OK, mucker!' I told him.

When I woke again myself, he was already awake. Must've been for some time, God love him. He'd sat there, hardly moving hardly, his wee nose pressed against the glass, not wanting to wake me. Bored out of his skull he must've been. When I said to him, he made out it wasn't any bother – had been good watching the different cars and trucks.

We freshened up in the toilets, then set off again. I'd to put my foot on the gas, I had to. When we entered Germany, the officials let him stamp the Blue Book and T-forms. We could expect more hassle in East Germany, I told him – though it wasn't as bad now, wi the Wall down an' that. He'd seen it on TV alright. The Berlin Wall. Folk dancing on it.

We both agreed it was brilliant.

'Best of it was: there was no violence, son. That's what they always shouted: *No violence!* That and: *We are the people!* People o Northern Ireland could take a leaf out of their book, mucker. *We* could do wi some people power too. Get rid o that Thatcher, for a start!'

He looked as if he was surprised. Hearing me talking like that. Then the wee bugger put on a TV voice and gave it: *That was a Party Political Broadcast on behalf of the Paddy McEvoy Party!*

Wee joker!

On the road down, he spotted signs for loads of towns with UEFA Cup teams. We talked about the Tic being out of Europe again. Damage was done at Parkhead, I said. 'Aye, ye can't afford to lose goals at home,' he agreed. 'Keepin your opponent out's half the battle.'

After that, we talked about the Autobahn. I was able to tell him the crucial differences. No speed limit, for starters. Also: I wouldn't be able to drive a load like this on a Sunday. Only perishables. Fact you can get hills on German motorways. That you can have trees up both sides – something our planners wouldn't allow. I could see him taking it in, all. We settled back to watch the Germans drive. Way no-one hogged the fast lane. Way they used it to overtake, then pulled in again.

He commented at one point about the leaves and bits of branches on the surface.

'You'll make a smashing driver!' I told him. 'Some day you can drive me!'

It just came out. I was glad it did but. Meant I could see us still doing stuff years down the line.

I'd a surprise for him I hadn't let on about.

When I took the next exit, he looked at me as if he'd missed something.

'That us there already?' he asked. 'Thought it was *East* Germany??'

'Naw. Special treat! This is where I take my break always – '

Something I discovered once. A tip I could've passed on but didn't but. It's not as if you're not entitled to a break. There's always some bastard thinks ye shouldn't be enjoying yourself but. So I keep it quiet.

'A leisure centre!' he realised. 'Excellent!'

'Got trunks with you?'

'Got football shorts!'

'Grand.'

We went in and up to the counter.

'*Ein Erwachsener und ein Kind, bitte!*' says I.

Ye want to have seen the wee bugger's face!

I put my arm round him.

'You'll like this, son. It's got everything!'

Leisure centre wasn't the word for it.

We got changed and headed up, past the area with sunbeds, and round the back of the cafe to the pool. I'm heading straight for where I want to be, of course, having been often before. He's hardly able to put one foot in front of the other but at times, he's so gobsmacked. The facilities are amazing, right enough. There's the youngfellas his own age too but, doing all the stuff him and his wee pals would be doing – only wi a strange lingo coming out of their mouths.

I jumped in – whereas he stood at the shallow-end, looking. Taking it all in, I suppose: windows on three sides, the trees, the lawns, the moon. Folk outside. December, or not.

'Come on in! It's 32 degrees!' I shout.

He's cautious, walks down the steps. Something going on there, I think to myself.

We swim the short lengths together. Turns out he's an okay swimmer – no champion. Occurs to me I don't know who taught him. Least I never threw him in the nearest dam and left him to it, like my da did me.

You should've seen his face when the *Bademeister* turned the rain on and there was a light shower as ye swam back into the shallow end.

When we were ready, we set about trying everything. Swimming from one outdoor pool to the next. Relaxing in the whirlpools – the different sections of different pools on at different times. I told him to watch out for the salty one.

Back indoors, we came across a wave machine. Again, he was standing – all hesitant – at the edge.

'Are ye not goin in?'

'Aye – after you, maybe!'

'Ye jokin? Ye'd get me shipwrecked in thon, mucker!'

I knew not to make an issue of it. Raced him to the flumes

instead. He'd great fun on all the different ones. Not one of them frightened him. He even got me to do the Canyon.

After that, it was the steam-room and the JODINHALARIUM.

'The iodine's supposed to be good for colds,' I told him.

You could hardly see in the mist.

Someone screamed next door.

'I'm away out, Da,' he said.

I could hear something was up. He was for leaving whether I joined him or not.

'What's the matter?' I asked.

'Minds me of summit,' he says.

He wasn't saying what. Again I didn't push it.

Bit o sorting out to be done there, I thought to myself just.

'Let's go and top up our sun-tans!' I said. No more than that, at that point.

I could kick myself when I think o the stunt I tried to pull next. All cos I knew what the score was behind the next door.

I'd had time to think about it an' all, God knows I had. All the time I was in the solarium, sure, my eyes were fixed on the wooden doors wi SAUNA on the handles. Wondering how to get rid of him, I was – me that had just got him back! All cos I knew it was kegs off soon as ye entered that door.

I tried to buy him off with icecream. 'Tell ye what, son!' I says. 'You get an icecream from that machine an' I'll nip into the sauna there for ten minutes!'

Least I didn't buy it to him, hand it to him, and bugger off in –

insisting it would melt if he followed!

The youngfella looked at me just. Was right to, an' all.

'It's not for youngfellas like you,' I tried to claim.

'But Da, there's been younger boys than me going in and out.'

He was right, of course. Was what he said next made me realise the fool I was.

'Be fair, Da,' he says. 'Don't leave me on my own. I don't speak the lingo, remember?'

'It's not as if I do, is it?' I tried to claim.

'No' half!' he laughs and imitates me: *'Ein Erwachsener und ein Kind, bitte!'*

I had to laugh myself and that was it. Was like us laughing in the truck again.

I ruffled his hair. 'Okay. Away on in wi me!'

Saying that, the youngfella still got more than he bargained for. It was all over his face when I pushed the door open and two lads my age were there, no towels or nuthin.

I pressed on.

'Show you round first, son,' I said, not wanting to make it an issue.

I pointed out the two saunas, the rail to hang your towel on, the different showers, the rest room. Then we went out to the fenced-in bit. He didn't know where to look again when he saw guys all ages on deck-chairs or wandering round. Youngfellas, his own age and younger, were in the garden too. One weeboy'd his trunks still on.

I made a fuss of the cold plunge. Partly to distract him.

We laughed at one boy struggling to get in.

'So wha'd ye think?' I asked.

'Looks good,' he answered. Sounded a bit unsure but.

He'll be alright, I thought. Give him ten minutes and he'll be fine.

It was my chin's turn to hit the floor when we went back in: a *woman* in white overalls was now around, wi a wooden bucket and ladle. She was goney be doing the *Aufguss*, obviously.

There was nowt else for it: o'er to the pegs and kegs off. Dominic followed me – hesitated a bit, I suppose – then done the same. I grabbed the towel, patted him on the head. 'You'll be alright. Follow me just!'

Inside, I draped the towel over a couple of levels. 'Sit you down there, it'll not be as hot,' I whispered. 'Just make sure your whole body's on the towel. Your feet an' all. They're strict about that.'

Your woman came in.

'*Grüss Gott*,' she said and poured four or five ladles on the coals. The Germans pretended to groan. Next thing, she was twirling the towel and the heat came at us in waves. Dominic turned and beamed at me.

'D'ye like it?'

He nods like mad.

When your woman was finished, the Germans clapped, shouting *Sue-Gaby, Sue-Gaby* – and she did more. Two of us clapped too.

I leaned forward, whispered, 'It's not too hot? It's OK to go out when she does –'

'Naw, it's great!'

Next thing, he's shifting round and sitting at right angles to me. His elbow's on my knee.

Across from us, a German father and son are doing the same.

'Don't know about you, mucker, but I'm heading out,' *I* says to *him* after a bit.

'I'll come with you!'

Outside, I scooped him up, threatened to fling him in the plunge. He was letting on to fight. I could see he was up for it but, so I chucked him in. Knotting himself, he was, when he surfaced.

I stood there pretending there was no bloody way I was going in. He played along.

'I'm coming to get you!' he warned and he was up the ladder and down the steps in no time. He was still laughing when he caught me. I let him pull and push me towards the steps.

'*Hey! Ruhe hier!*' an old German moaned. '*Scheiss-Engländer!*'

I was happy to let the English take the blame. Dived in from where I was standing. Drownded the old guy, just about.

Dominic was straight in after me – killing himself.

God knows what his mother would've said if she'd seen us.

When we returned to the sauna, three guys were speaking French.

'*Il fait chaud ici, n'est-ce pas?*' Dominic blurted out.

I just looked at him.

A Frenchman laughed. 'Ja, ja, zerr 'eiss 'ier!' he answered – not realising Dominic's Irish.

'*Je m'appelle Dominique* – '

'*I scheisse Jean-Michel.*'

They shook on it.

Dominic turned and grinned at me. I had to laugh.

'Cocky wee cunt!' I said and clipped his ear.

It was dark-dark when we set off again. Wasn't far to the border now, I told him.

'Wouldn't've been able to take you this time last year! They were stricter then – '

'Will we see much of the revolution, Da?'

I'd to laugh again. 'What are ye expecting? Guillotines? Naw, son. You'll have seen more excitement when we used to go over home in the summer.'

'Why'd they put the Wall up in the first place, Da?'

'To keep capitalism out, mucker.'

'What's capitalism?'

'The opposite of socialism.'

'And what's that?'

As much use as a dictionary, I was being.

'Och, never mind, son. Folk are totally browned off wi the two of them, anyway.'

He shrugged. 'Take your word for it.'

At the border, a handful of guys in grey uniforms went through the motions. They looked lost. One had a GO WEST sticker on his clipboard. We were through in no time. In the moonlight, the deserted barracks wi their smashed windows looked a nightmare but.

As we moved off, I pointed out the hut they questioned me in the year before only. Told him about their pals taking the lorry apart. You weren't allowed to take as much as a newspaper in.

It was weird. You looked at it and didn't know whether to think of before or now.

'Can I ask you something, Da?'

'What?'

'D'you think they'll get together again?'

'Who?'

'The two – ' He stopped. I could see he was thinking I was thinking he was really thinking about his mother and me.

'The two *Germanies*,' he said.

It was in East Germany he finally told me about the shouting-match on Friday night. There we were, driving along – we'd seen the aftermath of five crashes in the first hour alone, Schweppes bottles and blood all over the joint at one of them – and he finally begins to open up. There's me, having to watch – the roads are made of concrete, are cracked, sandy, unfenced, there's not so much as a petrol station, sometimes no sign-posts either – and finally the youngfella starts to come out with it.

I ended up feeling I could kill that shite, Seamus. I told Dominic so. Asked him not to turn out like that one.

'He's too much like I was, son. That's what's wrong with him.'

He was quiet for a bit after that. I wanted to break the silence – could think of nothing to say but. It wasn't a problem but, I soon saw.

Every now and then, to show I was glad he was there, I reached across and patted him. He smiled every time, God love him.

At some point, I held out my hand.

'Put it there, mucker!' I said.

He took it and shook it. Way he did, I could've bursted out crying.

'Thanks for letting me come, Da,' he said. 'I'm really enjoying it.'

'Good!' says I. 'Did you enjoy the leisure centre then?'

'Aye. It was brilliant – Fandabbydosy!'

He paused. Then said something I'll never forget.

'Da, know how when ye hard-boil an egg and run cold water on it and it cracks and ye shell it?'

'Aye – '

'That's what I feel like now!'

Eejit me thinks the youngfella's hungry.

'Are ye hungry, mucker?' I say. 'Don't worry. We'll be stopping soon.'

'Naw, that's what I *feel*-like feel-like,' says he.

the beam 4

It would've been the early Seventies again, probably – '72, say – and Liam would've been on the verge of moving up to the big school – aye, that would be right. And it would've been a Sunday cos they only ever went there cos there was a lovely wee Irish priest in that parish – well, that and the fact one of his father's brothers and his wife had moved over now as well and they were living there.

Randall & Hopkirk was always on, Liam minds, while the egg & bacon rolls were being made. His mum had got him interested and now he was hooked. He loved the idea of Marty, all in white: popping up behind the baddies to warn Geoff. Beat guardian angels any day!

Anyway, one of them Sundays after Mass – at most the weans would've been out playing, in the garden behind the tenement – Liam was asked, and this was something that never happened, to nip along to the shop you could see from the living-room. He minds it being a wild long street, starting in front of his uncle's door, practically, and there was nothing, nothing at all, on the left hand side, and houses just – upstairs/downstairs affairs – on the right. The main thing, apart from the length and the straightness, was the whiteness of the road and the height of the pavement. It was more that sort-of sandy dusty concrete whiteness, not grey paving stones, not black tarmac. The place probably wasn't finished yet, that's what it would've been – that's why there was nothing to his left. That said but, it was all so run-down, so rough-looking – the vandals had got to it – you couldn't imagine them bothering to finish it now. *They woulda done it long ago if they were going to do it, that's what I say* was what his uncle said.

Anyway, it was a fair dander to the shop, even if you could see it from the window, not that you'd've thought anything could happen, specially wi his mother and father keeping an eye out, supposedly. Just as Liam was nearing the shop but – he's in his Sunday best, mind, cos they'd been at 12 Mass, and Sunday best at the time probably meant a shirt, all pink and purple and mauve, wi a tie from the same cloth – just as he's nearing the shop, as I say, there's these four youngfellas, same age as Liam or thereabouts, and one of them's black and his wrist's done up in plaster of Paris. Another one – Liam senses it coming, sort-of – steps out to block his path.

'*He* says you're to touch his stookie' this boy says, nodding at the black guy.

Liam seizes wi panic. He's only half-caught what the boy said. Can still tell there's more to this than this but.

'You're to touch his *stookie!*' the boy repeats.

'Aye: *touch* it!' growls another.

This time, to be helpful, the black guy holds his stookie out.

Liam reaches to touch it and the black guy slaps his face. He doesn't get past without being tripped up an' all.

Next time Liam sets eyes on the guy is at secondary school, the one he has to attend for two years before the top twenty-five are creamed off. Liam's in 1A and the black guy's in 1C – and though Liam recognises him immediately, it's not mutual. Ask Liam now and what he'll tell you about the black guy is there was one day – and this was at the age of twelve or thirteen – he saw him, egged on by others, challenging the fit wee shite they had for P.E. – and he managed to out-dip him on the parallel bars, he did, before making the Master look very silly, very silly indeed, doing pull-ups on the beam. Liam minds the boy – who went second and had a fair whack to do even to *match* the Master even – just hanging there just, and going up and down, up and down like a yoyo, nay tother a' baw, easy and steady as ye lik – and the Master, fair play to him, able to take it, shaking his head just, and laughing.

5 broken peaces

Kathleen McInally had hardly breathed her last before she was off to see what Kevin buckin junior – her own Kevin's eldest – was up to. Only she minded that Uncle Ted and Aunt Edna had come all the way from Boston, and that her brother Brendan and his wife Lizzy had travelled over to Derry from Sheffield, she wouldn't've stopped for that last look at them all – gathered round the hospital bed – even. They were breaking their hearts, so they were – not that she knew what they were bubbling for. Wasn't she the first in a long time to die o' oul age?

Kevin, when she found him, was in Regensburg, about to teach for the Fräulein using his mug back in Falkirk. He'd a pile of weans' jotters in front of him. She was pleased to see he was a lovely-lookin youngfella still – his father all over, a McInally. His hair was too long to be teaching in, that was the only thing.

She'd no sooner got there, Kathleen, than a woman – a bit older than Kevin maybe – arrived to show him to the classroom. Kathleen followed to get the shock of her life: the Quiet Man, it turned out, was a natural: all smiles and jokes. He'd the weans hanging on every word, was in and out of the rows, shaking hands even. You'd've thought he'd popped in for a cuppa, for God's sake, and not to teach them.

He hadn't half come out of his shell, she was glad to see. She was heart-sore too but, watching him. She could see the youngfella was happy as Larry, knew what phone call he'd coming to him but. Why the hell had they not made up? She'd tried telling Patrick even, her youngest, to tell *their* Kevin to *tell* his Kevin she was broken-hearted. Ten years they'd not spoke. Afraid he'd go to pieces, she was, when word came through she was dead.

Today's topic was 'False Friends', Kevin had just announced, when Kathleen snuck off to check on his mother and father.

Her own Kevin and his Maureen were at a public phone in Altnagelvin. Maureen, all tears and snotters and tattered tissues, had just got through to Scotland.

'It's bad news, love,' she told one of her weegirls. 'Your Granny died twenty minutes ago.'

Kathleen could hear *Coronation Street* on.

'Here's your Dad now!' Maureen said.

They must've asked was he okay.

'Aye, don't be worrying, I'm fine,' he said. 'I know me Ma's gone straight to Heaven, sure.'

Her Big Son's words, lovely though they were, were enough to give her a nervous-bloody-breakdown. She wasn't in Heaven at all! She was in a phone box at Altnabuckingelvin! That's what she got for being in such a rush to find Young Kevin!

Taking a deep breath, she told herself to wise up. She'd all Eternity, sure! And anyway, she'd like to see St Peter trying to keep her bloody out! After all the running to Mass she done –

Kevin's mother and father had the fingers dialled off them, trying to get through to him. *Hier ist der Anrufbeantworter von Rosa und Hans-Jörg Hasenkrug* they kept hearing. Problem was: the youngfella was renting a roof-space and the family downstairs wasn't in. Kathleen tried standing over the phone, was damned but if she could get them two to leave a message.

The last time the phone went, she got back to find Kevin in his underclothing just – tartan, if ye don't mind! – and drinking from a bottle. Gulping it down lik an animal, he was. Ye'd've thought there was no glasses in the house.

He sat down at his desk to mark.

Watching the youngfella was amazing. She could never've imagined a master being gentle, marking. He was pleased when the weans were right, and even where they made mistakes, he'd smile and write some comment. Was as if he'd the wean sitting next to him. She couldn't believe his patience. Had to be his granda he took it after. Certainly wasn't her – or his father.

Time was moving on. There was no sign of the people downstairs still, and Kathleen was browned off getting, watching Kevin mark. There was nothing out the window, only trees. Least, back home, the Troubles gave you something to look at.

She considered dropping in on her wake – the body'd be home by now. She couldn't stand the thought of them all puffing away lik chimneys but in her sittingroom. Nor could she be annoyed watching them pray for her. God knows she'd said enough Hail Marys in her own lifetime, without listening to themmins all. Naw, she was better off seeing what the craic was here. If she waited long enough, sure, she might find out was Kevin courtin even, whereas if she went back home, she'd get all het up, just, at her saucers being used as ashtrays, or at Mickey Adams from up the street stuffing his pockets wi sandwiches.

Late in the afternoon, so late Kathleen was amazed it was still open, Kevin went back to the school.

The weans in the room this time weren't weans at all: they were big lumps o youngfellas and weegirls, sprawled all over their desks.

The master, a mere slip of a man, goodlooking but, introduced Kevin. They'd been studying Northern Ireland for weeks now, and Kevin – born in Derry or Londonderry (the man said both like he knew what they meant) – was going to tell them about the *everyday reality*.

Nothing against the youngfella, Kathleen had to laugh but. Sure Kevin hadn't set foot in the place for over a decade! She wondered what he thought he was goney tell them?

She felt lik yer man in *Randall & Hopkirk* as she plumped herself down to listen.

Was a good job she was dead already, or she'd've had a bloody heart attack. The wee shite began by insisting he was Scottish now. Not Irish. He'd grown to adulthood in Scotland. Them was his very words: grown to adulthood.

To begin with – to capture their imaginations, lik – he described holidays in Ireland when he was their age – younger, in fact. He told them about the boat over from Scotland, the car journey from Larne. About the army, the sandbags, the checkpoints. He told them what he'd seen from her livingroom. The shooting, the stone-throwing. Stressed how terrified he was when his mammy sent him to the shops: 'Imagine!' he said, 'the first soldier I'd've had to pass would've been in my granny's garden.'

Kathleen took a dander out to see the looks on the German

weans' faces. She was amazed Kevin could mind so much still – and could tell, to listen to him, it wasn't as far behind him, all, as he thought.

'Can you imagine that here in Regensburg?' Kevin asked the class. 'Having to walk past armed soldiers to go to the shops?'

'Perhaps in the Hitler time,' one weegirl answered.

Shortly after that, the youngfella's voice started shaking. Kathleen could hear it. She could see he noticed himself, God love him. The weans were noticing an' all maybe. He was trying to pretend it wasn't; ye could tell to look at him he was vexed but.

She went over to put an arm round him, only to discover she couldn't no more. She watched the weans – their reactions – instead. The weegirls looked lik their hearts were going out to him. The youngfellas but were edgy – very edgy.

The Quiet Man of the Family was fairly talking now – for someone who never opened his mouth, used to. God was her judge: he'd the talk for another row of teeth suddenly, Kevin.

'When I was going back and forward late in the 70s,' he was saying, 'things seemed normal. Before the Hunger Strikes, lots of people *on both sides* wanted peace. The majority were sick of violence. The problem was, and still is, however, that you have powerful, armed minorities *on both sides* who don't want peace. You've folk with vested interests, too. A return to normality tomorrow would mean those people losing out: *financially* – because with law and order restored, there'd be no more black market and protection rackets; and – *politically* – because so-called representatives would no longer get elected by whipping up their communities' fears. If peace were restored, all that power – both economic and political – would be down the drain tomorrow. And those boys aren't going to volunteer for that now, are they?'

The atmosphere in the room was changing. Kathleen could see it. Youngfella must've noticed himself. The weans, God love them, weren't enjoying this. Were looking shocked. What it was was: Kevin wasn't talking about his childhood no more. That's what it was had changed. He was sounding like a buckin politician, if truth be told, to be honest.

The longer the youngfella went on, the more bloody annoyed she was getting. She didn't care what anybody said: ye don't bad-mouth your own people lik that. No matter how bad things are, ye don't give total strangers ammunition against ye.

It was lik he was stickin a bloody knife into her – that's what it was lik

The start of what turned out to be his last bit was the most hurtful.

'The real problem, for me,' the wee blackguard went on to say, 'is that people in Ireland (and England and Scotland, for that matter) aren't brought up to be mature, articulate adults who can think for themselves. Their schools, families and churches don't seem to want that – not really. So instead of taking one long hard look at themselves, folk poke their noses in other folk's business. They shit-stir, gossip, squabble. That's on a personal level. As for the political: well, a whole heap of junk is passed down from generation to generation – on the Protestant, as well as the Catholic, side. How are the young people supposed to resist that?'

Listen to the bugger! He was as bad as his bloody father got!

There was no stopping him either: '*That's* what's really depressing – ' Kevin went on, 'weans are growing up in ghettos, knowing nothing but the Troubles. And way beyond the year 2000, they'll be passing all that bitterness and prejudice on to *their* weans and grandweans. My family was fortunate: we got out!'

'I'll buckin *got out* ye!' Kathleen muttered. Like everyone else, Kathleen McInally loved Derry. Was Derry through and through. Something, albeit, was telling her the youngfella'd maybe a point maybe. The Germans, certainly, were looking lik they agreed with him.

'*That's* what breaks *my* heart,' Kevin said, making her listen again. 'Ordinary people's lives are being ruined. Aren't being given a chance. And the thing that amazes me is how come, in the modern world, the situation's not solved once and for all? Look at any other trouble-spot and you'll see Lord This and Lord That flying over, attending talks, you'll see the Americans and the UN and the EU, even, doing what it takes to reach agreement. *Your* country's united again, and the Cold War's over. So why's there still not a hope in hell of peace in Northern Ireland?'

Nobody said anything.

'Why do ordinary, innocent people have to put up with all that?' he asked.

The tears were tripping her suddenly – she could feel them, Kathleen. The youngfella did so care about Derry. He'd a funny way of saying so, just. There was no doubting the passion but, the anger in his voice. Looking at him, she suddenly wondered was passion lik that allowed? Or could Kevin get shown the door for talking lik that? When the master stepped in but to stop him, it wasn't cos of that. It was cos it was hometime.

You want to have heard the round of applause the youngfella was given.

That evening Kevin got the message.

When he phoned home, Kathleen saw him not putting the big 5-Mark piece in he had in his hand. He didn't want to talk that long.

He didn't shed a tear either – not in the phone box, not when he got back to the attic, and not when he lay reading in the dark. Kathleen knew to look at him he wouldn't be attending her funeral.

Sure enough, when the librarian from the school looked in the next morning, he'd been nowhere near the travel agent's.

'Is it the money?' the lady asked. 'I can borrow you some Mark.'

'Thanks,' he said, 'there's no need. I'm not going –'

'But your grandmother died –'

'I know. But it's not the way you think it is.'

'It's like this,' he said, looking at her.

He said what he had to say. Kathleen'd the consolation, at least, it wasn't directed at her. The Troubles it was, he said. The Troubles on top of them emigrating. Nobody's individual fault, his generation was denied something but. That was what the bottom line was.

The German looked at him just. 'What if you regret it later?' she asked and leaned forward to touch him.

'I won't,' he said. 'I know I *can't* go. I couldn't sit through it. Not just the church bit, but the wake, the smoke, the drink talking.'

Looking straight at the lady, he was.

His father and grandfather would never forgive him. Deep down in her own heart but, Kathleen couldn't blame the youngfella. He'd be climbing a mountain or something – not teaching anyhow – as they lowered her into the ground. It was the way he was just.

In the meantime he was hugging and holding this German woman suddenly. So he *was* courting. Last thing she saw, his tongue, the dirty bugger –

Within a day or two, she was six feet under, Kathleen.

You want to've seen the turnout! They done her proud, they did. You'd've thought Derry City were bloody playing! She just wished all that money hadn't been spent on buckin flowers.

Other than that, she was happy. The remaining family hadn't taken it as bad as they might've. That was one good thing about burying two sons, God have mercy on them, and four of her daughters, God rest them, before she went herself: after watching them six hanging on and hanging on, her other nine, God love them, had learned to let her go, to pray for God to take her.

There'd been a time she used to say mothers should be allowed to see their children die. They saw them into the world and should be able to see them out. She'd changed her tune now. The Troubles were to blame for all them deaths. The buckin Troubles. Colum and Paul. Mary, Sheila, Bridie and Ann. They'd never've been sick lik that at them ages otherwise.

The last mourner was leaving the grave. Patrick, it was – her youngest.

She'd been let go. Time to pass through properly, it was.

She supposed she'd better get it over and done wi.

As she headed off, she spotted young Kevin – up an Alp in

winter sunshine. He'd a lovely smile. She stopped to bask in it, and something told her the same smile would greet the ceasefire. It wasn't far off so it wasn't. She hadn't lived to see it but it wasn't far off but.

PEACE! Imagine! She was over the moon for the youngfella. Didn't begrudge it one bit. Next thing she knew but, she was seeing something else – an Austrian handing him a paper. An unopened *Scotsman*, it was, the front page full of a bomb attack. The boys were at it again, seemingly. She seen him an' all, alone that Christmas Eve for some reason, breaking his heart in Playa del Ingles. And she saw the reason why: a headline, upside-down, on a stand across from his table:

ULSTER CEASEFIRE SHATTERED

Kathleen McInally had seen ebuckinnough.

It was *time*. Sure as God, it was. St Peter could go an' shite if he tried to stop her! She'd march right up to God Almighty himself, she would! And she'd give off hell! Just lik she always done wi the Corporation. She'd give off about the Provos, she would. She'd give off about the Loyalists. And give off about bloody Major and his lot.

Kevin, fair play to him, was right. What the hell did they think they were doing? Inflicting that on innocent people? Why, after all them years, allow them to think there was peace, only to take it back off them? She'd give off something rotten, she would! About the whole buckin lot of them. The whole buckin sham.

how on under God

Three years that was her, nearly, over in Scotland now. She'd still to set foot in Edinburgh but. Sometimes, back at the start, she'd thought Liam would suggest taking a run across, taking a run over in the car one day – a special treat, to cheer her up; then he'd started work but, and it had been no time before she herself had had to go in to have her youngest one. All them years she'd been reading about Edinburgh back in Derry an' all! Took her mind off the Troubles, it did. Fiona, her sister-in-law, had posted things across and Bridget had always thought the capital sounded lovely. She could just imagine the Gardens beneath the castle, Princes Street and all the shops, and the flower clock where couples met, aye, she thought that sounded gorgeous: the flower clock.

Fiona'd already seen it, of course. She hardly ever went but, even though it was no distance in the car. The two o them should take a trip over, she was always saying, it would get Bridget out of the house. Bridget knew that was a non-starter; that her Liam would never be happy wi them two off galavanting, leaving him with the weans. She could just imagine her and Fiona on the steps down into the Gardens but: admiring the flower bed and working out the time. Knowing Fiona, she'd come away wi 'Half past a daffodil' or 'Three minutes to roses!' She was a star turn, she was. A generous soul, too, type that would give you their last ha'penny. Aye, Paddy'd got himself a good one in her, right enough. They got on well, her and Fiona.

Paisley but, it had to be said, was no Edinburgh. God knows what had taken them to a place called that. Against their religion, it could've been. Thinking of you-know-who, she'd even asked Liam was he sure it wasn't? Liam'd just laughed and said *Don't be stupid* and he'd turned to some of the weans and said *That's a good one!* and *Did yous hear that one? Did yous hear what your Mammy said?* Then he saw how worried and maybe even upset she looked but, and said not to worry, *love*. Bridget had felt lik telling him to away and shite. She was sorry now she hadn't. If it hadn't've been for the weans, she might've.

Paisley: for a long time, she'd hardly set foot in the place. It was easier to send her eldest boy, Liam, on the bus. He was a good wee youngfella, fairly growing up now, she could rely on him, – and sure the girls in the electricity shop always commented on his beautiful handwriting when he signed his name. He'd only to open the door of the shop, for God sake, and they were saying what a lovely wee writer he was, how they wished *they* could write like that. God love him, he only ever shrugged and blushed. Didn't know what they were on about, he didn't.

She'd just do the uniforms now and then that would be them done. Sean, the wee bugger, she'd just spent the best part of an hour looking for his grey shirt again! That was the only problem: the uniforms. It couldn't be done on Liam's wage so it couldn't, way the weans were growing! For all Liam went on about her *pin money* and saying he paid more in tax than she earned, it came in handy when it came to the uniforms. Wee Liam wouldn't've had his blazer for starting back otherwise. Wasn't as if you could just hand them down either, not when her weeboys were more years apart than her weegirls. And there was Liam, for example, just started the secondary school and the only one at it. Another three years it would be before Sean followed – and that was if they didn't move house. Bridget hoped they'd stay put for a bit this time. She prayed to God they would. Sure they hadn't spent more than fifteen months in one house in the past five years, what wi Liam's job an' all. She'd even been carrying wee Orla, for God sake, when they emigrated.

She really wouldn't mind staying put now, and that was despite the oul bitch next door. God forgive her and pardon her for calling the woman that, but she brought it upon herself, she did. One look at the woman's face was enough to give you a headache, for Christ sake. Bridget's stomach went every time there was a knock at the door and the weans were out playing. Thing was: the woman's own two wee grandweans were bad wee buggers and more bother than the seven of hers put together – but naw, it was never that when your woman was at the door. For God sake, she'd been out again yesterday shouting her head off, making out the weans would break her window, and all they were doing was playing badminton. Bridget had had to laugh right enough when wee Sean held up the thing they bat about and pressed the feathery bit and said, 'Aye, sure, Mrs Henderson, this here's goney smash your window.' She'd had to laugh inside her; she forced herself to tell him off but. Not that it had helped: your woman had stormed off muttering words she hadn't heard before: she threatened to *skelp* Sean, a good *leatherin* was what he needed. Sean's face, God love him, had been a picture: 'I think she wants you to bate me, Mammy' was all he'd managed to say.

She was impossible, that woman was. Sure the only time Bridget had ever heard a kind word or a good word out of her had been when she'd got down on her hands and knees wi a pair of scissors last summer and cut all the grass. Couldn't've been done for years before, it couldn't. Ye had to hand it to the oul bitch: she'd got Valerie, her daughter, to loan Bridget a lawnmower once it was down to a decent length. Course it was no time (that was the thing about her) before she was out giving off again. It browned Bridget off, even if she only understood the half of what the woman was on about, what between her perforated ear-drums and the fact she couldn't catch the Scotch accents. Three years over she was now, and she still couldn't make head nor tail sometimes of what people were saying to her. Even wi her own weans and the Scotch tongues they were getting in their heads: sometimes she'd've needed a wha'd-ye-call-them-boys? – an interpreter.

God, this was great! That was an hour the wee ones were down, sleeping!

It was half three. She'd need to be getting ready for the twenty-past-four bus if she wanted to get to work on time.

It was getting better now, sometimes she even looked forward to it. It was company for her, apart from anything else – some of the Scotch girls had turned out to be quite nice after all. The only one she couldn't fathom was the one married onto your man that was teaching Liam English. Gin Kiss or something the other weeboys called him. It was just his nickname, that was the only explanation she'd been able to offer the youngfella. 'It's probably just his nickname, son. Just you call him Mr McGoldrick and you'll be all right'. She could see the disappointment all over his wee face but, when she said it.

The other youngfellas obviously didn't like the English master. Bridget didn't think Liam did either, ye wouldn't have got him to say so but, he wasn't the type to say anything, not even if ye asked him. The one thing she knew from your woman she worked wi was that the master had just retired from the army. They'd been over in Germany, and now he was teaching English. It was funny how they never spoke again after thon one time. Bridget thought it was even as if the woman was avoiding her though she couldn't think of a reason why. Then again, maybe the poor woman had gone home and he'd said he didn't want her talking to the mother of one of his pupils. Maybe he was even just plain embarrassed at the mark he gave wee Liam – the estimate of 19% when he missed the exam cos of all the strikes. Poor youngfella, having to explain that one to his father, even if it wasn't his fault. She couldn't mind how on under God he'd managed it.

Aye, it was grand now, right enough, now she was starting to understand the girls she worked with. And despite all the noise of the cans and the tins an' all! When she'd first moved over, God Almighty – even going shopping! She hadn't been able to catch what ones said to her at all. Even ordinary things. And to make things worse: they couldn't make her out, either. She was too Irish, they complained. It was wild embarrassing, so it was, when they asked her to repeat things and they still couldn't catch it. Some of the things they didn't know an' all: like *scallions* and *cooked ham*, for God sake.

It was no wonder she'd ended up sending the weans to the shops. Liam, her eldest, always went for the bread and milk – he could carry the five loaves and eight pints – and she'd send normally Ciara and Annette for the other things. She also sent Liam for anything at the Chemist's. The chemist would take the folded note and then hand over the prescriptions; or the giant-sized jar of *Sanatogen*; or the *Dr White's* wrapped in newspaper. God love him: youngfella thought he was buying firelighters!

The weans were far better wi the new money, anyway. She herself still had to think of things as *two bob* or *half a crown* or *ten and six* or whatever. Liam's mother'd been the same when she was over. The one thing Bridget did know was the pocket money: the big ones got two new p. and the wee ones one-and-a-half. It wasn't a lot, she knew, and they'd only been getting it since she went back to work, and they hadn't got it the week the uniforms were bought, but it meant the world to them, even if others in their class might've got five or even ten new p. It was funny seeing how some of them spent it, and what they spent it on, whereas some of them were more careful and would save it. Aye, they all had their own wee personalities, right enough!

They weren't bad, so they weren't, whatever the oul bitch next door might say. Bridget wouldn't've had it any other way. And they were getting so as they could be a help to her an' all. Not just wi the shopping either. There was young Liam, now. He would heat up the dinner for the rest of them all when he came in from school, and would give his father his when he got home. Him and Ciara were practically bringing up the two wee ones an' all: were giving them their feeds and putting them to bed. Aye, they weren't bad. Sometimes she didn't know what she'd do without them.

She was glad she'd started letting the big ones stay up a bit. She hadn't asked their father, she'd just done it. At first, Liam, her eldest, would've got staying up quarter of an hour, say, to help her wi the Paddi Pads. Then she'd let him see the end of *Coronation Street*. Monday night was his Cubs night, and sometimes when he got home she'd've let him watch *Colditz*, or *Dave Allen*, say. Now, if she was working and his father was going straight back out again, they were able to leave him in charge of the rest of them, even if, strictly speaking, he should've been sixteen. Even if they *had* been able to get hold of a babysitter but, that was another expense they couldn't afford, sure.

God, listen to her, she was as bad as Hilda Ogden getting, singing as she went about the house – her that never wanted to sing when there was a sing-song in Liam's mother's house an' all! If they'd let her sing *Little Arrows* or *Puppet On A String*, something cheery like that, it wouldn't've been so bad. But naw, it was always *Slievenamon* they wanted.

Right, she just had to get her overall, turn off the wireless, scribble the weans a note, and then that would be her.

Ding-dong!

Avon calling!

The front door. She looked at her watch. Shite! Who would that be? She hoped it wasn't the priest again. Was bad enough last week when he'd stopped her getting to her work. She'd had to slip next door to use the phone and call the factory to let on it was that time of the month and she couldn't make it. They'd said it was okay and not to worry. Lousy shites had docked her the day's wages but, rotten bloody sods that they were. When she told Liam, he said she should just've went and left the priest wi the weans. Holy God, even just the thought of it! Poor man wouldn't've known what had hit him! It had been embarrassing but, not being able to offer him anything, and her waiting off and waiting off, hoping he'd get up and go and – trust their Sean! torturing her with questions, 'Mammy, what's for the tea?' and 'Mammy, when are we goney eat, Mammy?' – and there was her trying to make out they never ate at that time cos she hadn't enough to offer the priest some. She could've wrung Sean's neck so she could've!

Thon was never a priest, thon was a woman at the door. Too broad to be Mrs buckin Henderson but.

The woman on the doorstep looked for a minute as if she thought Bridget was goney eat her, or something.

'Mrs O'Donnell?'

'Aye – I mean eh: yes – Can I help you?'

'I'm Mrs Colquhoun, Mrs O'Donnell, Senga Colquhoun – Pleased to meet you!'

The woman held out her hand. If she was pleased, she'd a funny way of showing it. Bridget shook her hand though she was none the wiser. Maybe it was just a neighbour wanting a cup of sugar, or something.

'Pleased to meet you, too, Mrs Coo –' It was no good: she couldn't get her tongue round it.

'Colquhoun! Do you mind if I come in for a minute, dear? I was just in with Mrs Henderson next door, and I thought I'd look in on you, too. I'm from the Council!'

Bridget's stomach went, inside her.

'There's no need to worry, Mrs O'Donnell, this is just a routine visit. We always drop in on our new tenants –'

Routine, ma arse. God forgive her and pardon her, but Bridget suspected Bitchface right away. The miserable oul bitch had reported her, had put the council on to her.

They passed the dining room on the way in. Bloody dining room: it had looked as if a bomb'd hit it. At least, she'd sorted the junk out and tidied it all last week. If this one'd seen the room in the state it was before, they'd've been in trouble now so they would've.

The navy-blue two-piece disappeared into the livingroom. Was as if she couldn't get in and out quick enough. As if she was scared of something. Did she think the house was a booby-trap, or something?

Bridget gave herself a shake and followed her. Trust Liam-bloody-Christopher not to be here when this was happening. Was the same last year when the bayleaf boys came.

'How many wee ones do you have, Mrs O'Donnell?'

What was she asking that for?

'Just the seven,' Bridget answered.

'Goodness! You don't look it – a woman your size – '

Bridget looked at the size of the woman from the council.

'And this is a three-apartment, isn't it, Mrs O'Donnell?'

'That's right – '

'Do you find you manage?'

Bridget didn't know what she was on about.

'All those children – in a three-apartment?'

'Oh, that's no problem. Sure they're grand big bedrooms and we've got bunk beds up in them,' Bridget explained.

'Do you mind if I have a look?'

Speedy Gonzales was out through the kitchen and halfway up the stairs before Bridget could say anything. Ye'd've thought a bomb was under her. Bridget was just glad she'd changed the beds and got the washing out that morning. That was ten bob she owed St Martin, even if she hadn't promised it.

'I must say: you've got the house looking lovely, dear,' the woman said when Bridget caught up with her. She was in the front bedroom, fingering the bars on one of the two cots. Least she wasn't afraid of catching something. Maybe she wouldn't be reporting her, after all.

The woman must've seen the look on her face. 'Don't worry, dear,' she whispered. 'I won't waken the wee ones! As I say, the house really is a credit to you.'

It was lik showing Liam's mother round: what they said sounded like a compliment, ye couldn't be sure but whether it was or not. Not that she'd time to worry about that now: she was just praying your woman here would leave the house in the next five minutes, otherwise she'd miss her bus. Wasn't as if she could make out it was that time of the month two weeks in a row, was it? Bloody priest, last week, making her tell a lie! Whoever seen her at the end of this week, she might not be in any fit state to work. Would be then she'd be needing the day off.

She checked her watch again. Began to wonder what was keeping Ciara and Annette. Normally they were back by now.

Jesus. She just hoped nothing'd happened to them.

Your woman – at last, thank God – was on her way down the stairs. 'Well, I shan't keep you any longer, Mrs O'Donnell. There's clearly no problem here, none whatsoever, and I see you already have the evening meal prepared for your husband and children. That's lovely. Well done, dear!'

She held out her hand for Bridget to shake. The woman, in a way, was as nervous as she was. Or was raging she'd been given this job. There was something about her, anyway.

'I won't have to bother you again, Mrs O'Donnell. I've seen enough to know everything's under control in this household.'

She turned to go.

'Feel free to drop in any time, Mrs C –,' Bridget said, opening the door for her. 'You'll be ever so welcome,' she added in the poshest voice she could manage. Already, she was imagining how she'd tell Liam when she got home – or better still: Fiona. Fiona would appreciate it.

As your woman stepped out, Ciara and Annette came running up the steps.

'Sorry we're late, Mammy!'

'It's alright. Say hello to the nice lady, girls!'

'Hello!' they both said. Ciara even said 'How do you do', God love her, when the woman from the council shook her hand.

Your woman just said, 'They're two lovely girls, Mrs O'Donnell. You can be proud of them,' and went down the steps to where her car was sitting.

Bridget waited until the car pulled off before she made her getaway. She didn't need eyes in the back of her head to know Bitchface was at her window. She shouted to Ciara to play wi the wee ones in the playpen until Liam got home from school, then nearly broke her neck racing across the road and down the steps to catch her bus.

She made it.

It was on the bus that it hit her, that she realised she was so up to high doh she was shaking all over her and crying. She pulled her scarf up over her face and turned in to the window. She tried to force herself to think of something different, to think of something nice. It was no good but: all she could think of was maybe the clock in Edinburgh had hyacinths in it. She didn't like hyacinths. They went for her something awful.

She could see her reflection in the window even though it was filthy. Look at her for God sake: she was buckin desperate-looking. It wasn't fair – things lik this always bloody happened when she was on her own, when Liam-bloody-Christopher, damn him – God forgive her and pardon her – was nowhere to be buckin seen. It wasn't fair. It was as if she'd got a showing-up, even though noone was there to see it. Even when they praised you, now she thought about it, they made you feel lik – lik *shite* – even though you were doing your damnedest to keep things spotless, were working your bones into the ground.

The thing was: what would have happened, ay? what would've happened if your woman'd come this morning before she'd had a chance to clear up, when she was still doing the wee ones' nappies before putting them into the playpen? What if she'd found her Liam's cigarette ends on the toilet and the edge of the bath, ay? Or his shavings on the inside of the wash-hand basin? It was no good, no matter how much she prayed to Him, she didn't know how on under God, how the hell she was supposed to cope.

They were going to end up taking the house off them, that's what was going to happen if they didn't watch, that's what the oul bitch next door was wanting. And it wasn't as if they'd anybody to turn to, over here in Scotland, apart from Paddy and Fiona, that is, and they'd five of their own, wi another one on the way. For all she'd said against them all when they were back in Derry still – sometimes she couldn't see them far enough, and even now was glad of the Irish Sea between them and her – at least they could have turned to Liam's family or her own family over there but.

Naw, that wasn't right, not any more. If she was honest, it had never been the same after her Mammy died.

She needed another hankie.

Whatever happened, however hard things got, they were better off over here, away from the Troubles. That's what she had to keep reminding herself: the weans were better off over here, *far* better off.

The stop after this one was hers.

She told herself to catch herself on, to pull herself together. If she didn't, she'd end up doing herself an injury wi them tins.

Watch, she'd need to watch. Need to watch herself.

As she was clocking in, she let a laugh out of her. What Liam's mother had said had come back to her. Themmins over there, Liam's sisters, all, obviously thought her and Liam and the weans were having the time of their lives, were living in the lap of luxury. Bridget wouldn't've been surprised if they were jealous, if they held it against them. Sometimes, even wi Liam's mother, ye got the impression they thought you were traitors cos ye went away. Because ye'd left Derry.

Derry –

As she sat down, she laughed again – ye had to, hadn't ye?

She switched on her machine and heard the buckin click.

She looked up. Holy Mary and St Joseph: they were all staring at her.

five fingers strand 7

To let you understand: every summer, for years, they'd been going over into the Free State anyway – each year, whoever saw them, with yet another addition to the family – but at some point during the war they moved over, as it seemed to the weans at least, permanently. Watching them, it was amazing to see how easily the wee ones could forget their house in the Brandywell and settle as if they'd lived all their lives in the house with the corrugated roof. You should've seen it: they would hardly've reached the front door each time, for God's sake, before a whole team o them would be racing round the back to try and use the thunderbox first, and the next thing Dessie or Bridie knew, Young Dessie or Brendan or Mick or one of the younger boys would come running up wi a collection of dock leaves that would keep the whole squad of them in toilet-roll for a week. Aye, most of them, God love them, took to Lisfannan. The craic was good, sure, that close to the beach.

At most, Dessie and Bridie's eldest *girls* would've been put out. Certainly, there came the day they left school and started work, and the factory-horn then kept one or two of them back in Derry, with or without their mother and father. Youngfellas wasn't the problem, though; there was noan of them on the horizon yet, at least noan that Eilish and Patricia, glamour girls though they were, were admitting to. Naw, on the face of it, the Cassidys seemed to take evacuation in their stride, apart from the fact Dessie senior had to cycle back and forth between Derry and there to put food on the table. While it was true, you see, that him and Bridie had had more than the dozen weans it was supposed to be cheaper by, they could never've afforded to feed them all at Free State prices.

Still, the bike kept Dessie fit, like, and God knows he had to be cos many a night he was smuggling stuff across, he soon had a customs official or the Gardai on his tail and sometimes it took a hell of an amount of pedalling to shake the same boys off.

While they never ever caught him, Dessie was sure they knew it was him. You had to hand it to them but: they never let on they knew anything when he passed through in the daytime – in fact, Bridie, God have mercy on her, was the only one of the two ever to get a showing-up, the time she went through wi whole supplies of flour taped round her, trying to pretend she was eight months gone. The poor woman had no luck: didn't one of the customs men's wives mind that Bridie's last wee youngfella had been a Christmas baby, and so whatever it was she was carrying, it couldn't be a wean if it was thon size!

Other than that, the two of them had no real worries to speak of – or so they thought as their weeboys spent whole days down at the rock-pools fishing for sticklebacks and shrimps, and their weegirls played at whatever they played at on the beach itself or the steps leading down to it, interrupting themselves only to come up to the house for a slice or two of the scone bread that was always on the go, or for the creamed rice Bridie made from scratch. Aye, ye can understand them thinking they'd nothing to worry about alright as those long summer's days would have drifted into nights, and cards would've been played or there might've been a bit of a sing-song or the youngfellas, in particular, might've tried to outdo each other telling everybody the jokes they knew before Big Dessie would've clicked his fingers and said, 'Right! – Bedtime!', and if there was any objection, all he had to do was say, 'I'm counting to three!' and right enough, by the time he was saying, 'Two-and-a-half – ', 'Two-and-three-quarters – ', most of them would've been up the ladder and claiming a space on the mattresses beneath the roof; one or two of them might've tried to remain behind, to stay up longer, and Bridie would've pointed out that they – the 'Big Ones' – were growing up now, and Dessie would or wouldn't've let them away with it, depending on how he was feeling. He liked to keep even the older ones guessing.

II

There *was* a problem, and that was the eldest boy in the family, named after Dessie himself. When the war got bad, the youngfella would've been in his teens just, and it's not as if he'd brothers to look up to; only sisters he didn't talk to and who couldn't've helped him wi what he was going through, anyway. Back then, of course, there was things you didn't talk about. Who knows: if the youngfella had had older brothers in the same room at night or to go swimming with, maybe some things would never've become an issue the way they did. Dessie and Bridie, it has to be said, never began to suspect anything was ailing him, was eating away inside him – which is not to criticise them: sure when you've fifteen of a family, God knows: however much you love them all, the amount of attention any single one gets has to be limited.

And that's what happened: when young Dessie could've done wi a bit of attention most, God love him, his father was biking backwards and forwards like a lunatic, and his mother was either changing the nappies of her youngest ones or washing them. You can hardly blame Dessie and Bridie but: sure they thought the sun shone out of the boy's arse and had every reason to do so – hadn't the youngfella got through the Qualifying, the only one of us who did. He was being taught by the Christian Brothers in St Columb's College itself, for Christ sake – the first in the family, ever. All being well, and if it was God's Holy Will, the family was hoping he'd one day make a Science master.

It was in one of them wartime summers the same boy stopped – *not* going to Confession, that wouldn't've been possible in a good Irish family in them days; naw, it wasn't so much that as: he stopped *confessing*. There he was: he could just about've been a working man if it hadn't been decided he'd carry on wi the school, and he was still rattling the same sins off he'd come up wi for his First Confession: 'Disobeyed ma mammy and daddy, fought wi ma brothers and sisters, told lies, and stole a bickie when ma mammy wasn't looking' – thon kinda stuff. It's not as if the same boy wouldn't've had more to confess either: peeing into Sean Breslin's bottle of mineral after drinking some, for one thing; not looking away when the wee spastic girl up the street, God love her, pulled up her jumper and showed herself, for another; and above all: him and Mickey Devine dropping their drawers thon day up at Five Fingers Strand to show each other their thingmies (the story went round our class) and then what happened to Dessie's when he saw what thon rogue Mickey done, then Mickey pointing to the stuff on the sand and saying that's what wee babbies were made of, that bits of Dessie's Mammy and Daddy were in there, and of his grannies and grandas, and maybe even their grannies and their grandas – and when Dessie Cassidy, the poor youngfella, looked at him, shocked out of his skull, and as if God would strike them dead there and then, all Mickey Devine done was ask him where else then he thought the Cassidy Ears or the Devine Nose came from?

III

The Cassidys were unusual in Derry in that they were connected, or part of them was, at least, to Germans. Even at the height of the war, Dessie's gran made no secret of the fact but, sure it was Derry and not London they lived in, she was always saying. The same one didn't bat an eye when German prisoners were herded through the streets. Nor was she in the least put out when the scuttled subs glugged their way to the ocean floor. No way did that one let things lik that bother her.

It was the exact opposite, in fact: she often told Dessie – and then he would boast to us – about *her* gran, his father's great-gran, a Gerry who'd emigrated to London at the time of the Revolution – in 1848 – and met Dessie's great-great-granda. Dessie's gran always made out this woman was wild intelligent, maybe that was where Dessie got his brains from. She wrote books, apparently, or kept a diary at least, and seemingly they still existed, even, in the British Library in London. They were all wrote in German but, so it wasn't as if they could read them. His gran often said that deep down she hoped someone somewhere in the family – and God knows there was no shortage of grandweans – would take up the German one day and go over to London and read them papers and come back and tell them all in Derry what was in them.

Dessie, first time he heard that, thought maybe, for some strange reason, that was why his own mother was always torturing his father an' all: it wasn't just that she hoped thon Adolf Hitler would bate the living shit out of the English; she was also always on about what a good-looking man Mr Hitler was, and how if she'd been German it would've been him and not Dessie's father she'd've gone for, sure she only married his father on the rebound from her one true sweetheart anyway.

Getting his gran onto the subject of their German Connection was never exactly difficult, and whenever he did, the bit Dessie liked best was the bit about the High Chimney Policy. His gran minded his great-great-gran telling her about how where she came from in Germany (his gran couldn't say the name of it) the women used to bleach their bed-linen out on the grass – until the day, that is, the new factories came along and soot and other dirt started to flutter down on the washing they'd worked so hard to get white. It seems the locals wherever it was didn't take this lying down: they'd got their act together and gave off hell – and their petitions and protests meant the factory-owners had no option but to do something. All the boyos did, right enough, (and this was the bit that amused Dessie) was build bigger and bigger chimneys just – so the wind would carry the smoke and soot further and further away and the folk in the village nearest the factory had nothing to moan about.

It was them chimneys that stuck with Dessie as he grew up, as he felt something build up and build up inside him, and as it wasn't as if he could've talked to anybody, or done something about it, it built up until one day he felt what his own weans, weans he never thought he'd have, would later call *well and truly shafted*.

IV

Scotland was his penance, his retribution; maybe it was even a form of Purgatory in advance of his death. That's what Dessie Cassidy, God rest him, convinced himself of as his sixtieth birthday approached. It was God's way of punishing him. For years he'd been terrified God would strike him down early and leave Eileen to bring the weans up on her own, or that something really awful would happen to one of the seven thon wee wife of his had carried for him. No matter how much he'd watched but, waiting for thon pot to boil, nothing ever happened. Instead, his family all turned out lovely, enjoying success after success, so much so Dessie became convinced God was letting the balloon grow bigger and bigger just so there'd be a bang the day it did burst. It didn't. Dessie just got to realise his punishment took a different form altogether: all them years in Scotland, away from his beloved Ireland; not being present when his mother and then his father, God rest their souls, passed away; and only being able to watch as his own weans became oul Scotchies, lost their brogues and – God knows – probably their religions too. Not one of them married a Catholic.

Aye, it was God's way of punishing him – that's what the poor craitur convinced himself of. For years he'd thought because of the episode at Five Fingers Strand, the time him and the Devines went the run, that he'd never become a father. Instead, he fathered seven, only to see them turn out but nothing at all like he'd hoped on the day of each of their births. Fruit of his loins? They might as well've landed from a different buckin planet.

V

Why I've gone to the trouble of telling you all this is this: In 1994, at a funeral mass in Carfin, the priest was reading his eulogy for Desmond Michael Cassidy when one of the dead man's family rose, worked his way along the pew, stepped out into the aisle, and without genuflecting began to walk forward. Even before he reached the altar, he announced to the priest he'd like to say a few good words about his father. It was Dessie's youngest, John-Paul, the afterthought of the family, and the youngfella had already raised eyebrows that day by wearing an ear-ring. Maisie Donoghue hadn't been the only one to comment she didn't care how fashionable it may or may not have been, the youngfella should've shown his dead father more respect and left it off. John-Paul, upon reaching the altar, continued 'I'd like to – but I can't' and as he went on before an attentive or at least silent congregation to dispute the picture the priest had been giving of a *very holy man*, of a *pillar* of the St Vincent de Paul and the Knights of St Columba with a *special devotion* to the Virgin Mary and a *great love* of Mother Ireland, his Uncle Bernard, who'd travelled over specially, came raging up a side-aisle shouting he was goney bloody well kill the wee shite when he got his hands on him. The priest and all us ones in the congregation believed Bernard, too, when he said it. We hadn't reckoned but wi wee Mrs McAuley from up the street who'd a soft spot for John-Paul, he was her favourite of all the Cassidys, God rest her soul, and not even recent talk of him maybe *not liking girls* could do anything to change that. From her kneeling position in the pew, Mrs McAuley managed to hook Bernard's ankle – the right one – wi her crutch and the next thing everybody knew, the big lump was landing flat on his face at the seventh Station of the Cross. There was a silence as his forehead smacked the base.

God forgive us and pardon us but nobody moved to help the man: we were all too busy watching Dessie's oldest boy, Des, who stood up, hugged his mother, looked to make sure she agreed, and as he stepped out into the aisle – he didn't genuflect either – he turned to his wife, Moira, who was holding wee Scott, Dessie and Eileen's first grandwean, in the row behind, and he took her hand and squeezed it to assure her it was okay, that everything was goney be okay, then he walked up to John-Paul, put his arms round him and even kissed him, and when John-Paul hugged him back he hugged him and kissed him again, and he turned to the congregation and said 'John-Paul's right. Our John-Paul is right'. Then him and John-Paul went over to their mother and whether the Mass was ended or not, the three of them led the way out.

an allergic reaction to national anthems 8

No harm to Lizzy or anyone else, but it wasn't the Queen they waited up for but: it was the late-night horror film. DON'T WATCH ALONE was the name of it, not that there was a hope in hell of that – not wi a houseful of weans lik yon, there wasn't.

Aye, the craic them Saturday nights was something else, right enough. They'd all be sitting there, sure, watching it in the dark – wee Orla and Cahal would've been cuddled up against their mother or father or some of the bigger ones – and there wouldn't've been a cheep out of them, not a single one of them – until, that is, every time Dracula was about to bite neck, and their da would free himself from whoever he was sitting beside and creep up behind the settee that was pulled up in front of the fire, and drop his falsers out of his mouth and down the back of some of their necks. Ye want to have heard the screams out of them! Half the suspense would've been wondering which of them their da would go for next; and he would do it to ye even if he'd promised FAITHfully never to do it to ye again. Ciara, say, would be sitting there thinking she was safe, thinking he would keep his promise – she, after all, had been the one to make him a mug of tea – and the next thing she knew his slabbery oul false teeth would be tumbling down the back of her wee frock. Then THE END would come up – and it was strange going from that to the photo of Lizzy on her horse and

GOD –

SAVE –

OUR –

They never got past OUR- in the O'Donnell household. It wasn't as if the Queen got zapped wi the remote control either even. Naw, we're talking the days before remote controls here, when you had to get up off your backside, cross the room, and press buttons or turn a dial. Not that the O'Donnell weans let that stop them but:

NO WAY!

No matter how tired they were, sure –

No matter how late it was –

No matter how many o the wee buggers had dozed off on the floor or settee, claiming they were resting their eyes and refusing to go to bed –

Even if they were out for the bloody count, for Godsake –

Or if the wee-est ones were past their sleep and grumpy as hell–

I'm not jokin ye: when it came to the band striking up GOD SAVE LIZZY, the whole bloody clan of them would come back to life and race from whatever corner of the livingroom they were in and *descend* upon the poor television set, each desperate to be the one to reach the ON-OFF button first. 'CHRIST SAKE, WEANS!' Bridget would scream out of her as – yet again – holy hell broke loose. She'd visions every time of the TV set coming off the top of the trolley and down on top of one of them. No matter how much she looked at thon husband of hers for support but, he would only laugh – pleased to see he was succeeding in rearing his weans up properly.

In the early days, when the race to turn the Queen off was beginning to be a regular occurrence, one of the Big Ones would normally have beaten the Wee Ones to the button. Ye could normally have put money on Annette who was as determined and as swift as she was shy and quiet. Liam, the eldest, might've had a good head on him, he was no athlete but, no matter how much it hurt his pride not to win the race.

The same boy – ye have to hand it to him – could certainly produce the odd stroke of genius but. Even his father had to laugh the night the wee bugger sat within easy reach of the plug and – cool as you like – just whipped the thing out as the rest closed in on the set. Lousy shite: when the others realised what had happened and turned to face him, he'd his head back, laughing, was gloating and goading them: twirling the plug above his head, the bugger was, lik it was Mick Jagger's mike. Another night – Annette, hoping he wouldn't notice, had already installed wee Orla and Ciara to defend the sockets – he stood up and left the room as the anthem was about to start. To look at him, ye'd've thought he wasn't goney compete; that he'd decided the whole bloody thing was beneath him. Turns out he was on his way to the fuse-box under the stairs. The looks on the faces descending on the telly were a picture, apparently.

Rest of them were demanding re-writes of the rule book thon night, so they were. The wee chorus of 'and se-ent them home-ward, to think a-gain' from beneath the stairs was the last bloody straw. 'Daddy, tell Liam he's not allowed to do that, Daddy!' 'Mum, tell Liam that's not fair, Mum!' they chorused. 'Think you're a smart arse, do ye?' was all Annette said when Liam re-appeared, looking pleased with himself.

Aye, Annette and Liam certainly had their moments of glory, no doubt about it. If ye study the form over the months and years this carry-on went on but, it was Sean – Bridget and Liam's second boy and the reserve goalkeeper in the school team – who stopped Lizzy in her tracks most. The youngfella could be flat out on his back on the mat in front of the fire – and he'd still manage to turn and glide through the air, finger and thumb extended to steal the moment of glory from whichever of his brothers and sisters might have been ahead of the pack this time. 'Bonetti the Cat' or 'Pat Jennings the Second' his father would call him, laughing as the youngfella avoided the trolley and completed his victory roll in the kitchen, returning gulping from a pint glass of water, stopping only to hold it aloft. Ye had to marvel at the wee bugger's agility, his courage. It's a wonder, in fact, he never got hurt, way the rest of them would crash down on top of him. Still, it was good practice for the penalty area on Saturday mornings, his father supposed.

Naw, there wasn't oncet, not a single once, the youngfella shed a tear, no matter how often or what way the rest of the mahoods landed on him. Naw, if it ended in tears, it was more likely to be one of the Wee Ones, *inconsolable* at not being the one who'd turned the TV off. Sometimes, to pacify them, their mother or father would've had to turn it back on again for wee Cahal or Orla to switch off – and ye'd get a snatch of REIGN – O-VER – US before Lizzy was cut off in her prime again. Their mother or father intervening would put an end to the waterworks alright, normally. Ye could see deep down, but, that even wee Cahal and Orla, God love them, knew that their mother or father setting it up for them wasn't the same as getting to the set first in the first place.

It didn't help, of course, that one night, Ciara, the wee bitch, spelled it out to Cahal who she was in a huff wi at the time: 'Don't know what you're looking so happy about, ya wee cry-baby,' she'd sneered. 'Jist cos your daddy turned it back on for you to turn off again doesn't mean you stopped the Queen first. It was still Sean first, *even if* you got to do it, too!' That had started Cahal bubbling again so Ciara got a cuff round the ear, was sent to bed, and was told in no uncertain terms it would be a long bloody buckin time before she'd get staying up long enough to see the Queen again.

•

It was a different story, of course, when they were listening to Radio Eireann and the Soldier's Song came on. The fact the reception was rotten on their tinny wee tranny was neither here nor there. Their da had picked the thing up for something like 20 new p. at the school jumble-sale, and it stood on the mantlepiece with the aerial fully extended. Big Liam, whoever saw him, would've been footering about all night with it, trying to get decent reception: trying tricks like having the aerial leaning against the clock or touching the mirror. 'Ye wouldn't think it was just across the Irish Sea – ' was what he usually said. 'God's my judge: we got better bloody reception the night the Tic played Ujpest Dosza in buckin Hungary!'

Rotten reception or not, the Irish national anthem was allowed to play right through. It was rousing stuff, wi bits where ye could join in. All ye had to do was sing 'God – bless – them!' between the lines sometimes – as if it was a rugby or a football song. Not that Wee Liam, for example, did but. Not bloody likely! Even at that age, the youngfella was allergic, sure. No way could he've listened and, in his own mind, seen, say, footballers lined up, chewing gum and having a good scratch to themselves. Naw, even at that age, visions of raised rifles and men's heads in balaclavas would've got in the way.

The surprising thing is that the youngfella can't mind the words no more. What he does mind is his da getting to his feet in his tea-stained vest always: he'd still've had his tea in his left hand and a fag in his right, and he would've pestered the rest of them to get up off their arses, too. 'Show some bloody respect, would yis!' he'd say, tugging at their sleeves. There was something comical, right enough, about their da standing there, saluting the tranny, and trying to drag Liam or Sean up to do the same. Sometimes but, he'd totally lose his temper and claim they'd a buckin cheek calling themselves Irishmen – or even Celtic supporters! 'The macaroon bars and spearmint chewing-gum – that's all yis bloody go for! That's the only reason yis bloody go. Buckin macaroon bars and spearmint chewing-gum! Don't think I don't know!'

There was hardly a night they were up late, nevertheless, passed but without the odd one or two of them joining in – for the final chorus, if nothing else. The Wee Ones didn't know any better, and even they could recognise when the orchestra was coming to the end. The bigger ones would or wouldn't've, depending on the mood they were in. Annette or one of the other girls might've, I suppose, – if only to please their daddy. Certainly, if any of them had got into trouble during the day, it was well-known that joining in – or offering to make him a mug o tea – was a short-cut back into the good books. As for their mother: there was no way on this earth ye would've got Bridget O'Donnell singing. She was totally browned off wi the whole thing, was past finding it funny, and normally disappeared into the scullery just. Not that it mattered, right enough: sure when it came to the last line, it didn't matter how many were singing: they always took the roof off with that one.

•

There came a time, of course, when the older ones would've joined their mother. The fact their father cast it up to her, calling her a traitor and claiming she'd spent too long in England as a wean, wouldn't've stopped them.

Liam was in there, exchanging looks with her, the night the police turned up at the door. It was the night Northern Ireland beat Scotland one-nil in a friendly at Hampden, wi George Best scoring the only goal. It was their mother's first-ever football match, and her and their father had gone along wi another couple – from Limavady, originally. Bridget had been so busy talking to the other woman but, she missed the bloody goal. 'Never mind, sure I'll see the replay!' she'd said as Georgie and the rest of the boyos danced their way back to their own half. Their da had loved telling the weans that one. 'Never mind, sure I'll see the replay!' he kept repeating, tears of laughter flooding out of him.

Anyway, thon was the night the police turned up at the door, and the O'Donnells were still so over the moon at Northern Ireland beating Scotland, ye'd've heard them back in Derry. No way were they goney settle for singing the Soldier's Song just once that night: naw, even as it was playing on Radio Eireann, their da looked a single out that had it on the B-side – and he kept the arm on the record-player back so as it would play over and over again. Wee Sean – trust him! – was killing himself when he realised, and turned it up full blast, the rascal.

It's not a bit of wonder they didn't hear the bloody police! Liam and his mother wouldn't've heard them, for chrissake, if they hadn't been in the kitchen. Saying that, the two of them weren't even sure it was a knock, so Bridget had asked Wee Liam to go to the door with her. She nearly bloody passed out when she saw the two policemen – managed to say 'Go and get your Daddy, son' before they said anything but. Strange thing was: the police had actually waited for the man of the house. Must've seen the shock written all over the poor woman's face.

It was pandemonium, of course, when Liam opened the livingroom door. He'd to shout 'THE POLICE WANT YE, DA!' twice, for Godsake, before the rest of them began to calm down. His da said, 'What?' and Liam repeated it again. 'They're at the front door wi Mum,' he said, then marched over to interrupt the record. There was a terrible scratching kinda sound the way he did it; not that his da said anything.

The weans watched in silence as their da pulled his shirt on, quick. He was on the verge of leaving the room, when he stopped to put his tie on after all, and used the mirror above the fireplace to straighten it. Only oncet he was satisfied did he go out to face the music. The poor youngsters could only look at each other, terrified. Finally, wee Orla, God love her, couldn't take it no more and bursted into tears, thinking her mammy and daddy were going to be arrested. Annette had to comfort her.

Ye could've heard a bloody pin drop. Not a word was spoken as they tried to hear what was happening. All they were able to make out but was their daddy using his polite voice to do the apologising and explaining. 'I can assure you two gentlemen it won't happen again,' he said, then a policeman said, 'That's fine then, Sir. Good night then, Sir', and they heard the front door shutting.

Their mother and father came back into the room.

'Bloody buckin bitch next door!' was all their father said.

'May she roast in buckin Hell!' he added, after a minute.

He was raging, crying, nearly, and was still shaking his head as he sat down, so livid was he at what had happened. Ciara, her wee eyes filling up, God love her, was on her way over to fling her arms round him when suddenly he looked up and started giving the woman next door the vicky. Ciara stopped in total shock: She couldn't believe her daddy would do a thing like that. Michael Duffy had got four of the belt at school, sure, four *sore* ones, for doing that. She looked over at Annette. Annette just shrugged like she was helpless but.

'One-nil, ye bitch ye,' their da was jeering.

The more he did it, the more the colour was disappearing out of Annette, the quiet one's face. Her daddy was making things worse, just, by cursing. That was *two* sins on his soul.

There was no stopping him but. Their mother couldn't do nothing either. The stupid big lump was waving his fingers at the dividing wall, and he kept doing it just – wi both hands too – until his two arms tired.

'Buckin-one-buckin-nil!' he hissed, finally.

Bridget saw her chance.

'That's enough of that, Liam O'Donnell, in front of the weans!' she said.

Their da didn't take her on.

She turned to them instead. 'Right, folks, BED!' she said. 'NOW!'

It was only after the last of them had left to go upstairs, wi their mother following after them, that their da noticed the cackle and hiss of Radio Eireann after close-down. He was damned if he was going to stand up but and go over and turn it off.

'Knock that off for me, would ye?' he said when Bridget came back down.

9   strange religions & suicidal rabbits

'Cheer up – it might never happen!' the woman at INFORMATION said when it came to his turn. No *Good afternoon!* No *Welcome to Glasgow!* – like for other new arrivals. Stefan Schmidt, for once, was flummoxed. Part of him worried he hadn't understood; that his *Englischkenntnisse* were already tripping him up. The other part – if he had understood – wanted to remind this person of her position. The one thing he did know was: his *holiday feeling* felt fragile, suddenly.

'Whatever it is that's worrying you might never happen, Sir,' **MORAG BRYCE** went on to explain.

Something about her smile said she wasn't out of order. That her comment was typical Scottish; not an *Unverschämtheit*. He smiled *vorsichtshalber* at the 'warm, friendly atmosphere', the 'genuine courtesy', he'd read about. Decided not to correct her. It *had* already happened. What was troubling him was complicated, though. His English wasn't good enough. He'd only get bogged down. And anyhow: it wasn't what INFORMATION staff were *for*.

Even on the bus north, the morning's events continued to niggle away at him. Trying to imagine his last-ever shift hadn't helped. Not when it came to the bit. The fact he was flying to Glasgow should've helped. Should've. Okay, so he'd got on the plane and gone. And the thought he'd be getting on a plane had put a different slant on things – not least when Petra was perched on the toilet, with him sprawled out, waiting. At least, today, he'd not sunk into a mood as he lay on the sofa. He was making up for it now, though.

Here he was, in Scotland, still moping about the mess they'd made of saying goodbye.

What bugged him most was the memory of Petra in her wheelchair, flanked by *scheiss* Dieter and little Felix. Was as if they'd *lined up* specially. They'd chatted awkwardly, with everyone knowing they were avoiding the goodbyes, when suddenly there was a silence which Dieter punctured by sticking his fat paw out: 'Okay, Stefan – Bon voyage, ja?' And that had been it: cold, impersonal. Might as well've been *military* service Stefan had done.

Dieter had caught him on the hop. With that paw staring him in the face, it was as if it was he, Stefan, who was paralysed, not Petra. All he could think of was what he'd typed for her that time: *I wish, instead of abusing me, he'd go off into a corner and abuse himself.*

Stefan had known as he left it was an 'unclean break'. He'd hoped he and Petra would get it right, would say goodbye *well*. Instead, as he climbed on his bike, it was disappointed he felt. As he pushed off, it came to him why. He'd hoped, for once, she'd hug him.

II

The taxi took him to the door of the cottage: *Hamish's Cottage* – Stefan's for the rest of the week. The key, like he'd been told, was in the mail-box.

Inside, he gave himself a shake. Tried to jolt himself out of his mood. Even so, as he unpacked, he wished Jutta was with him. He consoled himself by telling himself that by doing the extra months, he'd saved a whack towards Phoenix. The pay was much better once your minimum stint was over. Now, he could fly to the States. Help Jutta home in August.

Looking round, he knew Jutta would like the cottage: the small, neat furniture, the fabric and colours of the curtains, the modest, stylish antiques. He couldn't complain: the place came with a fridge and a telly; a small radio, even. He liked the artwork. The owner had a thing about Schiele. A might-as-well-be-naked woman was in every room, nearly. There was original artwork also – which Stefan preferred. Etchings. Woodprints.

As he put the kettle on, he watched the hens. The window was level with the path out the back. The one cockerel was handsome: black, flecked with colour, though – and a blood-red comb. The hens were brown. One broke free with a worm in her beak, shook off the others, and scoffed it all herself. Stefan was still laughing when the cockerel came up to the window, as if to stare him out.

'I vant to sleep long tomorrow, yes?' he warned it. 'I vant to sleep wery long!'

On his first night in Scotland, a beer in a pub was a must. The walk into Dingwall was depressing, to start with, anyway: a case of one dead rabbit after another. Soon, Stefan was studying the corpses. One had been beheaded. Another, he could see, had tried to dodge the wheel. Another – he had to laugh – had put its head between its paws, shut its eyes, and *hoped*. The car had crushed its back. Hedgehogs were messier. Lay – squashed – in pools of their own liquid, looked like.

Stefan was beginning to wonder was it safe to walk here? In Germany, complaints would be made to the council. Folk didn't put up with health hazards. He focused, instead, on the roadside. On the grass, nettles, weeds, dock leaves. The thistles and dandelions. The fern, isolated bluebells, and foxglove. The brambles and hawthorn in the background. Chemicals weren't so damaging here, it seemed.

The last stretch of the walk was stunning. Was what he'd come for. He was looking onto the Cromarty Firth, his *Reiseführer* told him. Across at the Black Isle. The connurbation with the smallish towers definitely had to be Dingwall. In the slanting light, even the local hills, the fields with their various crops, looked special. On the horizon were peaks of mountains further south. More *significant* mountains.

In no time he was at the Royal, wondering where he could eat. The bus-stop in the side street was the one for getting back. It shouldn't be as far to walk if he took the bus to Evanton. A car passing with men in it made him do a double-take. The men looked solemn, in their hats, collars, ties. Shopping hours, Stefan knew, were liberal here. But surely – on a Friday night – they didn't do funerals?

The woman serving in the bar he entered asked too soon what he wanted.

'Just one moment, please!' he said and studied the range of beers. Guiness was the one he recognised, but he wanted something Scottish.

'You are having a Scottish beer?' he asked.

'McEwans do?'

He decided to risk it; nodded.

The barmaid had twinkly eyes, like all the girls up here. He was reminded of Frau Hemminghaus: the rhyme she'd taught them. *Tvinkle, tvinkle, little shtar! How I vonder ver you are!* Him and Rainer Vogts, always up the back –

'German, are you?' the man beside him asked.

It was what the guidebook said would happen. People spoke to you.

'Yes!' Stefan answered.

'Up here on holiday, like?'

The man's face was reddish-brown. Ultra-violet, it appeared, held no fear for him.

'Yes – for a week. And I like it wery much – with the exception, of course, of the dead rabbits!'

'Dead rabbits?' the man asked. 'Oh – you mean the country roads. Aye, we've a terrible problem up here with the rabbits, son!'

'I can see that. Bad drivers, too, *vielleicht* – perhaps?'

'Naw, naw! Aw no, it's not that, son. Not the drivers. Naw, it's the rabbits: suicidal tendencies, son. Ahm no' kiddin you: when they hear a car coming, they're all out on the road, *wanting* to die, *gagging for it*, screaming out of them in rabbit-speak, they are: TAKE ME!! – KILL ME!! – TAKE ME, – MISTER, MISSUS! – PLEEEZE!!'

Stefan didn't know if this was for real.

The man nodded, remained serious: 'Aye, we have to employ special shrinks for the rabbits up here, son!'

There was time for one more before the last bus back.

As Stefan waited at the Royal, the men he'd seen earlier walked past. They were wearing bowler hats. Overcoats, a round collar, a dark tie. Must be some sect, Stefan thought. It occurred to him suddenly they mightn't be English. American, they could be. Obscure. Mega-orthodox.

Two younger guys, totally out of breath, rounded the corner. Asked about the 25A.

'I am sorry. I don't know. I am strange here – ' Stefan answered.

'So are we!' they said.

He read the badges on their shirts: Elder Aaron Mailer; Elder Fraser MacDonald; Church of Christ the King and Latter Day Saints.

'I take the 22:57 to Ewanton, Balconie Street,' he said, to be helpful, then looked away. Being too friendly might encourage them.

Try as he might to blot them out, he could hear every word. Their accents were clearer than the Scottish ones. When he heard them joking about attacking the little boy on the bike coming towards them – 'You punch him – WHOOF! – and I'll grab the bike!' – Stefan couldn't resist challenging them.

'You are often having ewil thoughts, yes?'

The two elders laughed, embarrassed.

'Shit, he's caught us!!' MacDonald said to the other.

Mailer was quicker off his feet. 'Yeah, man, but that's why repentance is so good. It's so wonderful to *repent*,' he said – and performed a dance-routine, just about.

MacDonald had recovered. 'Yeah, buddy, *repent*,' he repeated. 'Hallelujah, man!'

Stefan waited till they calmed down, then looked each in the eye. 'I think, in order to repent – and to be *forgiwen* – you have really to be – how can I say? – repent-ING, yes?'

'Shit, he's got us again!' MacDonald said.

'You're a religious man yourself then?' Mailer countered.

'I think I not need conwerting,' Stefan answered. 'Is that what you guys do?'

'Yeah, we're missionaries!!' MacDonald volunteered, suddenly more confident.

'*Ihr könnt mich mal*!' Stefan thought. Guys were the same age as him. Were just out of school.

He had to say something, quick. 'Do you not find a certain *Widerstand* – resistance, I think – when you try? Most people have already a religion, no?'

Mailer agreed, but claimed they could offer 'something different'. He launched into an explanation about people starting off in Heaven, and God the Father sending them down through a veil – that was how you came to be on earth – and when you die, you pass through the veil again. It was all Greek to Stefan. His *Englisch* wasn't the problem this time, though, he reckoned.

Back in the cottage, he tried to continue his latest letter to Jutta. A page, say, before he hit the sack. It had been a long day, and was now after one back home.

He wanted to write about Petra: to commit something to paper. One good thing about typing her diary was: he'd learned from her openness. He'd never forget the first such thought he'd had to type: *In Dieter, an erection is not always a sign of erotic attraction; sometimes, as his eyes betray, he is anticipating a cruelty which he won't have the courage to perform.*

Stefan knew this line by heart, knew it *intimately*. But that was now. 'Don't blush! *TYPE*!' his brain had roared back then. In time, he'd come to admire this ability: to express her private thoughts.

To say how she was vulnerable. Even if her analysis was *extrem* sometimes.

What saddened me today, Jutta, he wrote, *was that it was Dieter, and not Petra, who said goodbye – even if she added 'Have a good trip!' I'd hoped it would be the two of us who'd say goodbye, without any formality, without the business side. She'd've had to initiate that. She didn't. Instead, I saw her trapped within his framework. I felt it, too. Couldn't reach across. And this was the woman I'd worked with so closely for eight months. The woman I'd lifted, carried, fed, bathed, dried. Whose hands I'd been.*

III

The next morning, he'd breakfast behind the cottage in warm sunshine. The radio in the bedroom provided music, the cockerel punctuating piano concertos with its cock-a-doodle-doos.

Sipping his Earl Grey, Stefan studied a map. Identified a loch within walking distance. He didn't expect much traffic on the Old Evanton Road. Looked out lanes and farm roads, even so. He'd carry just his guitar – and a book.

In Evanton, he stopped to buy a *Proviant*, then headed out the road that led to the glen. Even on minor-minor roads, he'd again to watch his feet. More *scheiss* rabbits.

To think this was Scotland! It felt more like home. The warmth of the air was incredible. He loved the slope of the fields; the gold of the wheat in the sunshine; the wooded slopes beyond. In one field, sandy-brown sheep were tight against a gate, so desperate were they for shade. Letters and numbers were stamped on their backs, like on crates. Stefan wished he'd a camera.

He was feeling better today, he noticed. The change of scenery had helped – the air, a good night's sleep. The *silence* in the countryside was so complete.

Jutta and his parents were right, he decided: he should make the most of this free time, even if noone could join him. After his *Zivildienst*, and before University. He'd never be so flexible again, would never be entitled to so many reductions. His parents were right, too, to head to the States while they could. The cost of Unification – the full cost – was definitely coming. People – despite Kohl's claims – would soon be bearing the brunt.

When he reached the loch, he had it to himself. Stefan couldn't believe it. In Germany, in weather like this, any lake or pool would be swarming. He dropped his stuff, stripped, and splashed his way in. Swam, floated, then swam again – for ages. Still couldn't believe he had the place to himself.

He'd decided to give it another five, max, when he suddenly thought he could hear singing. He turned in the water and – sure enough! – where his things were, four or five folk were arriving. Their songs sounded like hymns. 'Praise the Lord!' someone exclaimed when they finished. 'Hallelujah!'

Lord was *Herr*.

The people were just standing there, examining his things.

Stefan was treading water, telling himself – or trying to – that Christians don't steal.

These Christians were loud. Everything they said carried over.

'Oh look! It's all German stickers on his guitar-case!'

Stickers must be *Aufkleber*.

'Imagine a German, up here!'

'Aye, sure you get all the nationalities these days!'

'Maybe he'll play us something on his guitar?'

'Too busy swimming, by the looks of things!'

'As long as the youngfella's enjoying himself, sure!'

'God love him!'

'So, ladies! Are we going to take a wee dander round the loch?'

'We can do a wee bit, anyway, Frank, aye!'

One of the men was filming the view. For a moment Stefan was sure the zoom was on him.

'Let's move on then, ladies. Thon youngfella looks like he might want out of the water – and sure he could be naked for all we know!'

'Oh Holy God, Frank! Naked? You don't, surely to God, think he'd do that? And there was me thinking he was a lovely youngfella, a credit to the mother and father that reared him!'

Stefan couldn't believe he was hearing right. Whatever; he wasn't in the mood for letting this lot see. Frank could go and scratch himself.

By the time the Christians returned, Stefan'd forgotten them. He'd strummed his guitar a bit, then become totally engrossed in what he was reading.

When he noticed the others returning, he pretended not to.

'Oh look! Your man from Germany's still here!'

'He's put some clothes on but, thank God!'

'Are you going to film him, Frank?'

'Aye, go on, Frank! Maybe he'll play us a tune!'

Stefan, again, couldn't believe he was hearing this. He wondered whether to pretend he knew no English? Kept his eyes firmly down as if was reading. Not that that stopped Frank from tapping his shoulder.

'Hello, Deutschland!' he said and smiled, baring pipe-stained teeth.

When Stefan didn't respond, he went on, 'Deutschland? Germany?' He hummed the start of the anthem. 'It *is* Germany you're from, isn't it?'

Stefan, conceding defeat, nodded.

Frank laughed, with glee. 'See! You can't fool me! I knew it would be Germany you'd be from!' He turned to the others. 'I was right! It is Germany! It's Germany he's from! C'm'ere over! Come on! Mary! Maureen! It's all right – he won't bite!'

'What's your name, son?' Frank asked as the others approached.

'Stefan Schmidt.'

'Steff – Stefan! After St Steven! That's lovely, son!' he said. He turned to his friends. 'Stefan's the boy's name. Named after St Steven!'

'Stefan,' they repeated. 'Stefan – '

'I'm not wanting to disturb you or anything, son,' Frank continued, taking his book from him, 'but stand up a minute. I want to introduce you to some lovely people.' He pointed to the other man. 'This is a very good friend of mine, now. A lovely, lovely, very holy man. This is Sean Doran, from Galway!'

'Hi, Sean! You are not being Scottish?'

'No, Stefan, son,' Frank answered. 'Can you not tell by the accent, youngfella? No, we're all Irish. That said, my wife, Mary, and I – that's Mary there. Say hello to the youngfella, Mary! – my wife, Mary, and I live in Greenock, here in Scotland. We emigrated twenty years ago. Having said that, Stefan, son, we're as Irish as the day we came. It's something you never ever lose, ye know.'

'Naw, you never lose it,' the others confirmed.

'And this is Maureen, Sean's wife, and this is Orla. They're from Galway, too – well, Orla here was born and reared in Cork actually – but I want you to know, Stefan, and that's the point of interrupting ye, son, that I *love* these people!' Frank stepped between Maureen and Orla and put an arm round each. 'They're lovely, lovely people, Stefan, very sincere, very: pious, if you know what that means!'

'Pius was the name of a Pope, ja?' Stefan said, not knowing what else to say.

They all laughed. 'Aye, that's right, son. Pius was the name of a Pope. Pope Pius the Twelfth. Aye, right enough! Very good, son!'

'So you'll be one of us then?' Maureen asked.

'No, I am here only on holiday. I am from Germany!' Stefan answered.

There was a silence, then Frank put his arm round Stefan again. 'Stefan, son, I'm going to ask you a wee favour now. Will you play me a song on your guitar there so as Sean here can film you?'

The request seemed strange to Stefan. Life, though, he guessed, would be easier if he agreed.

'Are you ready, Sean?' Frank asked.

Sean lined the camcorder up as Stefan took his guitar out.

'What songs do you know, son? Do you know any English ones?' Mary asked.

'Oh, leave the boy alone, you. It doesn't have to be English, son,' Maureen said. 'You could do thon lovely wee one that won Eurovision – what was it called again?'

'*A Little Peace*!' said Sean.

They meant *Ein bißchen Frieden*.

'I can do English songs!' he volunteered, quickly.

'What's your favourite, Stefan?' Mary asked.

'*House of the Rising Sun*,' he answered.

Frank laughed. '*House of the Rising Sun*, ay? Naw naw, we can't have that. Not with these ladies present!'

'Do you know *I Am So Happy*, son?' Orla asked.

Stefan could only think of a disco song: *H-A-P-P-Y*.

'Naw, it's not that one, son!' Frank said. 'Listen and I'll sing it to ye, sure! It's easy enough. See if you can pick up the chords!'

Frank started to sing. The others joined in, clapping as they sang. 'I am so happy, as happy as can be – '

Sean was already filming.

Frank paused after the first verse. 'Have you got it yet, son? It just continues like that. The same again, except "Jesus took my troubles and nailed them to a tree," then back again to "I am so happy"!'

Stefan couldn't believe he was doing this. He strummed a few chords. They didn't seem to be listening, anyhow: so carried away were they, singing, dancing, clapping. Sean was making sure to capture it all.

'Oh, that was lovely, son. Thank you *very* much!' Maureen said when they finished.

'Aye, well done, son!' Sean said. 'You picked thon wee tune up rightly!'

'Do you know *Bind Us Together, Lord* ?' Orla asked. 'We could do that next!'

'I think I am having to go now! I have a long way!' Stefan said. He didn't manage to get past Frank, though, who'd his arm round his shoulder again.

'Sure there's no rush, youngfella! We can give you a lift to wherever you're going! And a gentleman like you wouldn't want to let these lovely ladies down, would you?'

'I walk villingly,' Stefan said.

'OK. But give us a wee chorus of *Bind Us Together* first, ay? Do it for me! Will you? Do it for Frank Kelly from Greenock!'

'Okay: I try. For a short time only, yes?'

'Agreed, Sir. Agreed!' Frank said. 'Sean! Have you got that camcorder going?'

What followed was a *Katastrophe*. Luckily, a middle-aged man arriving with a woman in a wheelchair interrupted things. Frank was over like a shot.

'Is this your daughter?' he asked the man.

It was. 'This is Marjory. Say hello, Marj!'

The man sounded English.

'Do you mind me asking what's wrong with her?'

Wrong with her?! Stefan was so annoyed he didn't catch the answer. He couldn't help thinking of Petra. Petra would've grabbed Frank's *best piece* by now, dug her nails in, and – ignoring his tears – insisted he address his questions to her; that she was perfectly capable of answering.

Marjory, Stefan could see, hadn't a word to say for herself. All *Marj* could do was smile. Hope they'd do her no harm.

Keine Angst, ich tu dir nichts, Stefan assured her, silently.

Frank was now on one knee in front of the wheelchair. He'd taken Marjory's hand between his. So-and-so wasn't just holding it, Stefan saw: he was *stroking* it. Stefan wished he could wish Petra's strength on Marjory. He couldn't. Instead, he could only listen as Frank said: 'The Lord gives us all a different cross to bear. But He loves us all – and invites all of us to join Him in the Kingdom of Heaven.'

Marjory didn't respond; maybe couldn't.

Her father looked floored by what was happening. He looked puzzled, that was for sure. Showed no sign, however, of wanting to stop Frank.

Frank stood up, suddenly. His friends stepped back, obviously knew what would follow. Frank rested a hand on Marjory's temple. He proceeded to pray, Sean making sure he got this filmed. Maureen nodded at the Englishman, then at Stefan.

'Frank's a wild holy man,' she assured them. 'He speaks in tongues. *And* he has the Gift of Healing.'

IV

That night, Stefan tried a different pub. It looked like a married couples' place. He hoped it did bar-meals.

He was hardly in the door before game-machine noises were deafening him. In Germany, he'd've walked back out. Here, he had to accept pubs were like this.

The clientele was surprisingly young. His own age, mostly. He took one look and decided to stick to his paper.

First, he ordered a pint. The people next to him were discussing crisps.

'Have you ever seen Gin Finn eatin crisps?' one asked.

Noone had.

'He takes a handful, smashes them in his hand like this – '

The others laughed.

' – then lobs them inty his gob like this!'

Everyone laughed again.

Grateful for the actions, Stefan laughed, too.

'Naw kiddin ye: he takes a haunful like this – smashes them – and then: up and inty his gob in one go wi' them!'

Stefan nodded to the two who'd noticed him laughing and went and sat down.

He took time over his pint, trying to suss the articles he was reading. He'd've given his right hand for a *Stern* or a *Spiegel*. You could forget international news in this country. Rest of the world didn't exist, it seemed. Bosnia and Rwanda weren't happening.

Instead, the papers were full of murders. Child murders.

Stefan decided he'd earned another beer. Asked for a small lager.

'A *half* pint?' the barmaid checked.

A man interrupted before Stefan could answer.

'You can't give a grown man like that a half pint, Moira. Make it a pint – and it's on me!'

Stefan recognised the taxi driver – from the day before. 'Oh – hello!'

'Hi again, son! Having a good holiday, are you?'

They chatted. Talked their way through the local sights: towns and places worth seeing. When Stefan mentioned being a keen walker, Ewen, the taxi driver, was able to give him tips.

'Did a lot of walking myself, son. When I was still on my own, like. Got a partner now, of course. It's different when you've only yourself to worry about. You can just take off – '

He asked whether Stefan had a girlfriend.

'Yes, Jutta.'

'And would she not come with you on holiday, like?'

'She's in the States. Doing a gap year, I think you call it.'

'That's not much use to you, now, is it?'

'I support her. It is a good thing to do. Though I miss her. Wery much.'

'I would miss my Irene, too, son – like a sore head!'

Stefan looked at him, astonished.

'Joke, son – *joke*! I love her really – like my own mother. I do! Anyway, I'll have to be leaving you. She'll be waiting for me. Nice talking to you, son!'

'Nice talking,' Stefan repeated. 'And thank you for the beer.'

They shook on it.

Stefan glanced round before he returned to his paper. Next to no impact he'd made on the pint Ewen'd bought him. The young ones in the pub, he saw, though, were fairly knocking them back.

Trying to make sense of 'Notes & Queries', he was, when he became aware of someone standing over him. He looked up. A girl, far too fat for the clothes she'd on, had her head tilted back – as if she was looking behind her. Her eyes, though, were focussed on Stefan.

'See her over there in the corner?' the girl asked, eventually.

'Eh – yes,' Stefan answered, unsure what might follow.

'She wants to know if you want to snog her!'

'What *snog* ?'

'This is *snog*!' she answered – and her tongue was in his mouth before he knew it.

Stefan broke free. 'You are tasting of fish and chips!' he objected.

'Single fish, actually!'

When he said nothing more, she challenged him again. 'So, do ye want tae? D'ye want tae snog oor Linda?'

'Tell Linda I have already a girlfriend in Germany,' he said, lifting his paper to go.

The two guys in the group made to block the exit. Next thing, they were approaching him, as if prepared to reason.

'D'ye no' want tae come an' join us, mate?' said one.

'Aye, mate, why don't ye come an' make it a six-some?' the other suggested. 'The girls want tae meet ye!'

'We could share an' share alike if ye want, mate – make it three each. Three burds, instead o' jist the one, like!'

They were drunk.

'I have to catch a bus,' Stefan said. When he tried to leave, the taller one blocked his path. 'But they're gaggin for it, mate. Really got the hots, ken?'

'Ur ye no' game furra shag, mate? They really want tae shag, ken?'

'What is *shag*?'

'Fuck!' the tall one said. 'I give up!'

'Fuck?' said Stefan. 'You call it that?'

He left, pushing his way through a clash of elbows that had no follow-up.

'Fuckin shirtlifter!' one shouted after him.

'Aye, poof was probly hopin' it wid be five each.'

Stefan got to the Royal to see his bus heading off.

Scheiße.

He'd take a taxi. The four-mile hike – six or seven kilometres, maybe – didn't appeal. The driver chatted away. He'd been on holiday in the Spring. In Spain – visiting ex-pats. If it wasn't for that, he wouldn't go, he said. He wasn't interested in Europe.

Suddenly, the car stopped.

'I think we are not there yet?' Stefan asked.

'No, no, we're not there yet, son. I think I hit a rabbit – '

The driver reversed a bit. There was a bump. A slight one.

'That's it definitely dead now. – I prefer to put them out of their misery.'

The car pulled off again, moving up the gears.

'It's mercy-killing, really!' the man explained.

As soon as he got into the cottage, he turned the radio on – but after a few minutes switched it back off. Either Wagner or Weill, it was. Or shock-jocks and listeners talking over each other. Poor reception, into the bargain.

Stefan put the kettle on. Sat down to write to Jutta.

It was good to formulate thoughts for someone who wanted to read them. Sometimes, he felt himself grinning, even.

I miss you, he wrote, finally.

He put down his pen and went to lock up – late-night rituals already established.

He considered sleeping on top of the duvet, then slipped, naked, beneath it. The duvet settled as he got himself comfy. Nestled into his chest.

First time he had sex, that had surprised him: the light trace of her fingers down his body hair, even.

He felt himself stiffen. Turned onto his front. Shifted the weight off his dick and went out like a light.

10   going, going

You'd've thought it was a major attraction or something, judging by the number of folk hanging round the top of the O'Donnells' garden. Even cousins who hadn't set foot in the house in the three weeks Liam and his family were there, were standing at the gate. 'Honest to God,' his gran had complained, 'I see more of yous, and that's yous three years over in Scotland, than I do of ma grandweans here in Derry.' Liam found that hard to believe, but his gran had persisted. 'D'you see that Majella Duffy one out there, for example? She's got a bloody cheek so she has, coming up today. She never comes near me, you know.'

Other cousins of Liam's were hanging round the car. Sean, Hughie's youngest, had already run up to Liam about half a dozen times and tugged his shorts and asked, 'Liam, are you going on the big boat, Liam?' Liam's 'Aye, Sean' in reply had probably sounded more impatient each time, that hadn't stopped Sean but from skipping over to his mother who was trying to talk to Maisie Cassidy, and tugging her apron and saying, 'Mammy, Liam's going on the big boat, Mammy,' and she would answer, 'Aye, son, that's great, son, isn't it?' while concentrating, really, on the story of how Maisie had been sweating the night before on clickety-click, sixty-six, for the big Snowball.

Liam and his family were leaving from his grandmother's house in the Creggan. Liam had wasted no time in getting out to the car when it came to time for going. It wasn't just that he was scared stiff the army might come round while they were putting their things in the boot. It was also because he felt the buckin tears coming. He could hardly believe it: he'd hated this holiday, absolutely detested it, had been terrified the whole time, and here he was on the verge of tears when it came to time to leave.

On his way out of the house, Liam had whispered in his da's ear to *please* make it quick. His da had stopped and looked at him. Then he said, 'Aye, okay.' He seemed to realise Liam was vexed. You could never get his da to shut up talking and just *go* but, so Liam was sitting in the car, looking up his gran's path, willing the rest of them out, and nabbing a brother or sister or two into the big green Zephyr when he could. 'Come *on*, you.' It was annoying when one of them slipped back out again.

His cousins weren't going anywhere. Most of the boys were around the car. Sometimes one would tap the bonnet, as if he knew everything about it. Liam might've been sitting in the Zephyr, he realised listening to them but he was stupid when it came to cars. He prayed they wouldn't ask him anything. His older cousins pretended to be authorities on the journey to Scotland as well – as far as Larne, at least. They were wearing Ben Sherman shirts, Wranglers that Liam would've said were too short for them, black socks and black brogues. Only hardmen would've dressed like that in Scotland. Noone in Liam's class at school would've had their hair short like that either.

Eugene, there, the same age as Liam, was suspected of throwing stones at soldiers. Someone had told his gran and she'd phoned for his mother to come down the street immediately. Liam's Aunt Margaret had come and Gran had told her. Margaret denied it. 'Naw, Mammy, our Eugene doesn't throw stones. I'm telling you, Mammy.' Gran said that wasn't what she'd heard. Soon Margaret was crying nearly. 'Naw, Mammy, I'm telling ye, Eugene doesn't throw stones. None of mine throws stones. They know what would happen to them if they did. They know I would take the belt to them.' Gran had let it drop, for the moment. The next time Margaret dropped in for a cuppa but, Gran was soon saying – in front of everyone – about that one there's Eugene out throwing stones. Margaret, in no time, was in tears again nearly. 'Naw, Mammy, I swear to God, Mammy, he doesn't. Sure that last night you said that, I went straight up the street and asked him does he throw stones. I said: now tell the truth, you. Do you throw stones? And he said he didn't. He said: Naw, Mammy, I don't throw stones. And I told him what you said. I said: Well, that's not what your Granny O'Donnell heard. And he denied it. He said: Naw, Mammy, I don't throw stones at soldiers, and he turned to our Paul and he said: Don't I not, Paul? And Paul said no, they didn't throw stones at soldiers. God forgive me, but I even took the belt but to the both of them, mother, and I said: Well this is what you're going to get if I hear you're throwing stones, and they were squealing out of them, so they were, and it was: But Mammy, I don't throw stones, and: Mammy, me neither. Mammy, STOP IT, Mammy, that's SORE. I ended it but by saying: Well just make sure you don't.'

Gran had let it drop again. As soon as Margaret went out the door but, she turned to Liam and said, 'You know, Liam, your Aunt Margaret's a big softie, ye know. She'll believe anything them weeboys o hers'll tell her. And she'll come down here and tell me they don't throw stones and she'll even say she bates the pants off them. I know different but: they do so throw stones.'

Looking at Eugene now, Liam could just imagine him throwing stones at soldiers, like all the other youngfellas in the street. What worried Liam was what would happen if the soldiers caught them.

Godsake, what was keeping his mother and father? If they didn't move their arses quick, the army would be round again. The bottles and stones would be flying. And the soldiers would fire rubber bullets.

Liam knew the Provos hid on the roof of the community centre there, sometimes, to have a go at the foot patrols. One of his sisters, he saw, was crying cos they were leaving.

By the time his mother and father did make it out, past his father's umpteen brothers and sisters and their husbands and wives (there was only three not married now), Liam himself was in a state. It was his sister's fault, he couldn't hold the tears back when he saw her. His cousin, Fatima, a big lump of a girl, was in the car beside him and crying her eyes out as she tried to comfort him. Liam was surprised by that. He hadn't realised they were that close.

His mother and father were in some state, too. He was amazed at his mum cos it was mainly only his father's family that was seeing them off. As for his da: even though he was breaking his heart leaving his brothers and sisters, Liam saw how in the end he practically shoved them out of his way to get to the car. The tears were tripping him, and it was as if he was looking down, looking away, already not wanting to see anybody any more. His da wiped his eyes and his nose on his sleeves, even, as he got in, despite the fact he was always telling Liam to use a hankie.

Before they left, Liam'd to get back out to give his grandmother a hug. 'Liam, you've not given your gran a goodbye kiss yet, son,' his mother said as she got into the car. She turned round, rested her chin on the passenger seat, and looked at Liam till he opened the door and climbed out. He walked round the back of the car. His gran had moved in behind the others, just like she always tried to hide in photographs. Liam could see she was putting a brave smile on. It was obvious she'd been crying, but now her lips were pursed and she was forcing her cheeks into a smile. The tears but were flickering in her eyes still. Liam wished she'd let them go just, instead of this act she put on.

111

He knew she always took her famous *brandy balls* when she was afraid of being upset. 'God love her, the poor thing wouldn't've got through it otherwise,' his mother was forever saying.

As he walked up to his gran, still sort-of crying himself, Liam heard Maisie Cassidy saying, 'Would you look at that wee craitur, he's breaking his heart, God love him.' 'Aye, his Granny's blue-eyed boy,' another neighbour answered. It was news to Liam, that. He stood in front of her, this tank of a woman in a purple-and-pink-striped pinafore. Liam had noticed the size of her the Saturday night she stood at the sink doing all the spuds and all the veg for the Sunday dinner. She liked to get them done the night before, she said. Liam had been the only other person in the kitchen and had sat in front of the lovely and warm stove, wi her talking the whole time, telling him stories. Afterwards, they'd played *Scrabble*, just the two of them.

Liam looked down. Gran was wearing her famous wee brown shoes as well, he noticed. She was always making out he'd be too ashamed to be seen walking beside her if she was to wear them over in Scotland. It didn't matter how often he said he wouldn't. They looked at each other; reached for each other. His ears were soon wrapped in his gran's pinafore. Even so but, he could hear Maisie Cassidy saying she'd never thought she'd see the day when Liam O'Donnell (she meant Liam's father) would leave Derry.

His gran didn't let go for ages. He felt her sort-of shaking, crying probably. Once he came round himself but, he tried to concentrate on Maisie again who was claiming it was his mother she felt sorry for. 'When you think about it, sure there's nothing for Bridget O'Donnell over in Scotland. God love her, stuck in the house wi all them weans and not a one to help her.' Liam felt right and angry. Maisie didn't know what she was talking about. Sure him and the rest of the weans were always trying to help Mum. He listened to his gran instead. She was saying something about him having been given his father's name and his grandfather's name. 'You're my oldest O'Donnell grandson. Don't you go losing your roots.'

Don't you go losing your roots now. How often had Liam heard that in the last three weeks? They all kept slagging him about his accent. He was turning into an oul Scotchie, they said. That hadn't stopped them asking whether he'd ever come back to Derry but. That was their favourite question: Would ye want to come back to Derry?

His gran let go. Something made Liam wish she'd said these things to him sooner. It would've been good to know sooner he was her Number One Grandchild, even though his da's big sisters all had loads of weans, and one of them was married already and had his own first wee one. Maybe him and his gran could've done more together in the three weeks they'd been over if he'd known. Liam had noticed that most of the time it was as if he'd been a *spectator* just, as his gran ran the show from the other side of the room. Everything in the house depended on her. On what she said.

For a moment he thought it would be nice to stay longer after all.

He promised her he would write, then walked round the back of the car. As he was about to get in, a car pulled up wi its horn tooting. It was his da's clown of a sister, Orla. Her short dresses and late nights drove her mother up the wall. Gran was forever throwing her out and letting her back in again. Orla called Liam over. 'Is that you off? Give us a kiss then!' she said. Her window was down. He pecked her on the cheek. 'Naw, a real kiss, for God's sake,' she demanded. Liam stopped, wondered what she meant, then sort-of smacked her lips.

By the time he got back in beside the others and got them to move over a bit, Orla was dooking in his da's window and giving her big brother up cheek. She messed his hair, then looked at her hand, disgusted. 'Oooh yucks, still overdoing it wi the Brylcreem, Big Brother?' She sniffed at his neck. 'And I've told ye before: thon Oul Spice is rotten.' Liam noticed that his da let her away with it. He even sort-of laughed through his tears. He kissed her. Next thing, Orla was stretching across the steering-wheel to the passenger seat, 'Give us a kiss, Bridget, love. Honest to God, I don't know how you put up wi that big shite.' Then she was leaning over their da's shoulder into the back seat, 'BYE, weans!' She put money into Annette's hand, 'You buy sweets for yous all wi that, love.' She was making out she was all cheery, Liam could see she wasn't but.

Orla tapped the roof and his da started the engine. 'Sure they'll be back, so they will,' someone was saying. 'Aye, if God spares them,' someone added. Any time anyone said that, Liam always wondered what kind of disaster might happen to wipe them out. He always stopped himself but, just in case God changed his mind and let it happen.

The big Zephyr started to pull off. Everyone was waving. Annette was waving, too, was telling the rest of them but that Orla had given them three pound.

'Three poun' she gave us. Daddy, Aunt Orla gave us three poun', Daddy!'

'Aye, very good. Give it to me and I'll keep it for you.'

In the wing-mirror he could see over his mother's shoulder, Liam now saw saracens pulling into the street. *Shite*. He turned and stared out the window. There was a new barricade they'd have to clear first. The bottles and stones were flying already. This was what he'd been afraid of. They were getting away just in time.

His relatives were hardly waving now hardly as they rushed

down Gran's path, or up the side of the centre.

'Place your faith in God just,' the Derry ones had all said, every time trouble started. Offended, they'd been when Liam looked feart. 'You don't believe in God enough, that's what's wrong wi you, weeboy.'

'Look at us, we place our faith in God and we're not scared.'

'And we *live* here.'

They were welcome to the place.

When he turned back round, Liam could see his father's face was like a soaking sponge.

The weans were behaving themselves, at least.

They headed for the cemetery before they left the town. His father took them to Granda Donnell's grave first. It was somewhere round the big IRA monument. As the car crawled along the path, Liam half-read the graves. It always said things like OUR LOVING SON, and then it gave the name, WHO WAS MURDERED BY BRITISH PARATROOPERS ON such-and-such a date. It wasn't exactly gravestone language.

His Granda Donnell had died just under a year ago. His da had flown home for a couple of false alarms before it actually happened. At least, when it did, his da was there. Liam minded his mum telling him – after seven Mass, it was. Liam hadn't cried. Not one of his brothers and sisters had cried, but then they were all younger. He didn't know if his mum had cried.

It had been days before his father came home. 'Uncle' Patsy went to the airport to fetch him. As soon as his da got in, he sent Liam to bed. 'Right, you, bed!' he said and gave the usual sign.

'What for?' Liam asked, though there was no point. 'For giving up cheek while I was away.'

Liam wondered what age he had to be to be past getting sent to bed. It was still happening.

Late that evening, his da had come up to the room wi a Polaroid picture of Granda in his coffin, looking so white, so peaceful. Someone'd had one of those new cameras. Liam didn't fancy the idea.

They found and stood at the grave. Liam had seen it before. They'd been sent photos to Scotland, enlargements, wi the big black stone in the centre and aunts and cousins on either side, in various combinations. Even Liam's da found it morbid, and it was his father they were standing round. His da knelt down on the rectangular bit of marble at the end of the grave and prayed. He'd one hand over his eyes, and the other, as if it was joined, at his chest. When he stood up, Liam's Mum knelt down. The weans all stood wi their heads sort-of bowed just. Cahal had his thumb in his mouth. Liam looked at the stone and thought, 'You'd've let us watch *Top of the Pops*.'

They went to Mammy Cluskey's grave next. She'd died when Liam was seven, a wee while after his First Communion. Liam minded waking up in the middle of the night and seeing his teacher wi the light on in the livingroom when he went to the toilet. She'd told him to go back to bed and not to worry. Then, just as it was getting light and the birds began to sing, his da had come in, seen he was awake, and told him Mammy Cluskey had gone to Heaven. Liam still minded crying all day, lying on top of his blue bedspread wi all the yachts. It had been hours and hours before his mother came home, and even then, she'd not done very much, not said very much; she'd just gone to bed to 'try and sleep'. Liam also minded the priest announcing his gran's anniversary a year later.

He hadn't realised until the priest asked the congregation to pray for Annie McCluskey 'whose First Anniversary it is.' Liam had cried all day again.

The white stones on his gran's grave were from him. He'd collected them and brought them back from the beach a fortnight ago. His mum had asked him to when they landed and saw the state the grave was in.

Liam hardly saw his Granda Cluskey after his Mammy Cluskey died. He just minded the first visit weeks and weeks after the funeral. He'd had to keep asking when they were going to go. The day they went, the usual big bowl of salad was on the table for them all, except it didn't have hard-boiled eggs in it. Liam minded slipping from room to room, looking for his gran – and then stopping, and hoping that would mean she was still in a room he just hadn't been in yet. His mum had wondered what was wrong when he refused point-blank to go through to the kitchen. She didn't force him.

His mum had been allowed that day to take any of Gran's suits she wanted out of the wardrobe. The one wi the fur collar still had Gran's hankie in it. Liam minded sneaking a smell at it.

He knelt down beside his Mum and managed a prayer. When his Mum had finished, she hugged him before she stood up.

His da said it was time to go. As they walked away, Annette asked Ciara did the coffin lids keep the water out when it rained or did Granda Donnell and Mammy Cluskey get wet? Ciara said she supposed so, that's what the lids were there for. Annette wasn't satisfied but, and pestered their da. 'Do they, Daddy? Do the lids keep the rain out?' Their da answered that yes, they did, but that it was no odds cos Mammy Cluskey and Granda Donnell were already up in Heaven. Liam wondered how his da knew that.

As they got into the car again, Liam realised they were going back to Scotland without saying bye to Granda Cluskey. His da mumbled something about no time now. Liam felt guilty about not saying cheerio to him. The last time, when they'd actually moved to Scotland, they'd found his granda in the Cathedral, and his mother had brought him out to where the car was parked beside the Clergy House. She'd got back into the car, and Granda Cluskey had stood at the driver's side wi his hands in his pockets, not even close enough, and he'd looked down and in and said cheerio and 'Well all the best then.' Him and Liam's da had hardly taken each other on. Liam had thought they were just too vexed.

'You'll send me that money?'

'Aye, of course, we'll send you the money.'

'Don't forget, now.'

Liam didn't know what that was about. His da didn't sound best pleased but. And off they'd went.

On the way to the boat this time, Liam watched his mother and father and wondered were they okay, were they going to be okay? He kept an eye on his brothers and sisters too, was glad they were behaving themselves. When anything did start up, he tried to sort it out, to calm things down, before his parents noticed. Just before Larne but, Sean started playing up and wouldn't listen to Liam, and it served him right when his father turned round and hit him two slaps on the bare leg. He was being totally inconsiderate.

Sean, Liam remembered, had let a soldier show him how to look down a gun, down on Marlborough Road. Honest to God, that weeboy would talk to anybody. He could've got them tarred-and-feathered; or knee-capped.

On the boat, Liam was allowed to go up on deck on his own. His da would take the rest up *after*. It was because Liam was nearly thirteen, his mother told the others.

Up on deck, he looked at the harbour. It wasn't up to much. A bit shabby. He watched the water as the boat pulled away. The distance made him feel sort-of sad. He wasn't going to cry again but. He was too busy thinking about things about the past three weeks he mustn't forget. Plus, he'd bread for the sea-gulls. A stale loaf, part of.

He broke the bread and hurled it into the air. It was strange. It was as if he was angry. Anyone watching wouldn't have known was he feeding the gulls or trying to hit them.

I know what! he decided. As I fling each chunk, I'll shout out loud inside myself the things I've left behind!

'CHECKPOINTS!!'

This was great fun!

'BARRICADES!'

Christ, I nearly took the head off a gull wi that one!

'FOOT Patrols! SARacens!'

Two bits of bread went whizzing off towards three gulls. Liam laughed at their wee fight in mid-air.

'Rubber BULLets! STONE-throwing!'

He'd watched rubber bullets land in his gran's front garden. One had broken in half on one weeboy's back as he ran towards their front door.

'HOUSE-raids!'

The women rushed out and blew whistles and battered their

tin bin-lids off the pavements when that happened, Liam had heard of soldiers taking their rubber bullets back, off of mantlepieces.

'BOMBscares!'

'Hey, did ye see that, mister?' he said to the man standing nearest him. 'It looked as if that first sea-gull back-heeled it for the other one to catch!'

The man laughed. 'Jist as long as they don't start dribbling all over the place, ay, son?'

Liam laughed, too. That had been the last piece. It had been worth it but. The best thing was: no matter how rotten his aim was, the sea-gulls swooped and caught whatever he threw at them.

He was noticing the wind more, now he'd stopped throwing. He shivered a bit.

The worst thing about Derry, apart from the bin-lids, had been having to walk past soldiers, and wonder was there going to be shooting, when his mother sent him for the bread and milk.

Liam hadn't told anyone yet, maybe he wouldn't do so, he'd decided but there was no way he'd ever set foot in Ireland ever again.

'Swear to God I won't,' he assured the good sea air.

a change of scenery 11

He closed the door behind them and leaned against it. Connor O'Doherty was now alone in his son's flat. It had taken a whole song and dance first but, right enough. After him getting up out of bed and driving the rest of them over for just after lunchtime as well!

You got no bloody gratitude. None whatsoever.

If he was being honest, young Brendan had made it obvious he didn't want him there, couldn't handle the thought of him being there alone.

That was the thanks you got for rearing them.

He'd only actually gone when his mother nudged him out, probably saying something like 'Offer it up, love!' or 'Do it for me'.

Typical.

Tough.

On his way back into the livingroom a draught hit him. It was blowing a gale through the flat. He went round closing the windows, stopping only to look at the bedroom again. There was definitely something about them bedclothes.

When he got back to the livingroom, he didn't park his bum where his son had made him sit. Not on your nelly, he was going to make himself comfortable in that one there – in front of the TV – instead. The radio was on in the kitchen still. He'd asked for it as soon as he'd come in and caught some of the comments and analysis before the matches started. If he was lucky, he might get a good race now on TV, the English results would come up at the bottom of the screen, and if there was any goals in the Scottish games, he was sure to pick up on it from the kitchen. He managed to get a picture up with the remote control. Good on ye, boyo! Aye, he could take to this. He was beginning to like the flat better, now there was a bit of life about it.

He got another fag going. There wasn't an ashtray so he took a dish from beneath a plant. God knows what the youngfella saw in plants anyway. It was like a bloody jungle in here, and it wasn't as if he'd a woman to look after them. That one there's a weeping willow, no – I tell a lie – a weeping fig, that's what it is. Aye, the old boy still knew these things. They needn't go thinking he didn't. They'd another thing coming to them if they did.

'And it's over to Parkhead where I think we have a sensational equaliser for Forfar Athletic against Celtic – '

'Yes, Tom, it's Celtic 1 Forfar 1 and – ' *Shite.* Connor raced round the door and turned the bloody thing off. It was the friggin board's fault. When he thought back to the Celtic team when he'd first moved over. All them years in a row. Different story these days. Buckin bucket team, getting stuffed week in week out.

He decided to make himself a cup of tea while he was there. Jaysus Christ Almighty, has he no friggin Tetleys like the rest of humanity? He found them. Bugger's got no milk but. You can forget the biscuits an' all, by the look of things. It's an English cup of tea you'll be having.

He sat down at the window to drink it, blowing over it first. Nice view out there, right enough. He could've sat all day, just watching what was going on in them other flats. He wished he knew how the young'uns managed it: how they put the money together for places like this. Changed days, so it was.

There was no sign of Brendan getting married either. As bad as his brothers getting. And he'd told his Granny, God have mercy on her, a lie. He always told her he'd be married when he was 23. The same one had known some lovely weegirls, too. Bernie had met them or spoken to them on the phone. Connor had told him, whether he liked it or not: *it wasn't right*. Sure when he was his age, he was the father of six – and Brendan was one of them.

Connor didn't agree with this own-flat business either. In his day, you stayed wi your mother and father until you got married, full stop. He'd told his weegirls what would happen to them if they got pregnant. Or rather: what he'd do to the youngfella, more like. It was different with the boys. Still against their religion but.

Ye wouldn't think this was him in Edinburgh! He would rather be back in the house, to be quite honest.

Now he thought about it, he'd never been one for travelling. He'd never set foot out of Ireland before they emigrated, sure. And all the years he was in Scotland, he'd never went anywhere, never saw anything. Well maybe the Supporters' Bus to away games, you don't see much that way but. The inside o the Hibs before you left and that was about it.

This country couldn't begin to compare wi Ireland anyway.

Then, right enough, a couple of years ago, he'd gone through a travelling phase. Suddenly, he was up and out and around the country, visiting his daughters and sons-in-law. The wedding would hardly be over and he'd be away off to visit them. His daughters were chuffed, and it made him feel good. He took Bernie with him, of course, drove her everywhere. Folk thought it was lovely. That it did him good to get out of the house. That maybe he could handle it after all, if he got his voluntary redundancy.

The only thing about trips like that but was: you were always in somebody else's house. He wasn't comfortable with it being John's house, like. Or Brian's. You had to hand it to him but: one thing he always did was christen the bed in the spare room for them. The first night in whichever of the houses it was, and he would make sure him and Bernie did it. Bernie was always against it, she'd give in but before she'd let, say, Bernadette and John think they could hear them arguing.

Bernie was needlessly ashamed about it. Them was the very words he'd said to her: *needlessly ashamed*. 'Sure they know about these things now. They're adults – married!' he'd told her. Bernie's face had relaxed a bit when she heard that. 'And anyway, they're probably doing it as well!' he added. The poor woman had gone beetroot.

He himself had only laughed.

The horses. He should get back to the 3.45 from Newmarket, see if Limavady Laddie made it. 3-1, the boy was. Pity he'd not made the bookies.

On his way through the hall, he noticed there was no Holy Water font. It was the same in the boy's old flat in Airdrie. He'd gone to bliss himself on the way out and there was no Holy Water font. This flat was the same. Not a single Holy Picture to be seen anywhere. It wasn't right. He didn't want the boy losing his religion, people saying he hadn't brought him up properly. Not a single Holy Picture, by Christ. He would never've got away wi it over home.

Sometimes Connor wondered whether he'd done the right thing in taking the family away from Ireland. Troubles or no Troubles. Sometimes, listening to them, ye would never know his lot were Irish.

He sighed as he sat down. Still just the adverts.

He trusted his weegirls to go to Mass all right. He was sure they did, even if two of them had gone an' married Protestants, Scotch boys, after him always saying an' all about Irish boys being far nicer, and them always agreeing. As for Brendan but, he probably couldn't tell ye the name of his parish priest, never mind what the gospel was about on Sunday. *I* noticed he never went to Communion on Christmas Day. His mother did too, she just wouldn't admit it. The bugger hadn't taken him on at the dinner table but, when he'd said about hoping they were still all going to confession every fortnight, or had at least been in preparation for the celebration of the birth of Our Lord.

There's the boy who rides Niamh's Song now.

Some wee dander that is. They still weren't back. Must bloody well be climbing Arthur while they're at it.

It occurred to him maybe he should go round opening the windows again before they got back. Brendan could be funny about things like that. Them looks of his were lethal. Obviously didn't slap him hard enough when he was younger. That's what the mistake I made was, where I must've went wrong.

He started wi the bedroom first. The boy slept at the back, it would be quieter than onto the street at the front. Connor opened the door. Them bedclothes again. There was something about them. The colours. The pattern. Like he was advertising something. The

125

fact it was a double bed an' all. It was against his religion, would lead him into temptation. Visitors, Brendan had answered, cool as you like, when Connor asked him what he needed a double bed for. Then: Some of my best friends are couples. Cheeky pup. That was the thing about him. He was that secretive, worse than his older brothers getting, and yet at the same time he tries to tant ye, to tease you.

It was a nice Holy Picture he needed up there, above the bed, married or no married. A Padre Pio at least. Connor had been going to buy him a lovely crucifix thon time at Carfin, his mother wouldn't let me but. The arguments Bernie had given him, into the bargain! He was so a Catholic, he just didn't want stuff like that up in his house, she'd said. He didn't want to be shoving it down the throats of anybody coming to the house. I don't know, the way that youngfella thinks at times.

He wouldn't even let you give him the Praying Hands. Bernie had spotted these lovely Praying Hands for him when she was over in Knock herself wi Dawn and she was going to take them for him. And she was right, sure they could be Protestant Hands as well, so they wouldn't offend no-one, but no: according to Dawn, Brendan had said he wasn't having the Hands or even *Footprints* on his walls. Have you ever heard the like?

Jaysus, this window was a bugger. He didn't know how the boy got it open first thing every morning.

HOLY GOD!

he knew sometimes he thought he was seeing things, thon was a bare arse but, if ever he saw one, in thon there window over there!

JAYSUS, MARY, AND SAINT JOSEPH!

Connor retreated, sat down on the side of the bed furthest from the window. He tried to light another fag, his fingers were all over the place but. It was so, it was a youngfella taking a shower and he'd the window up as far as it would go. God forgive him and pardon him. Had he no shame, the bugger? It wasn't just his backside he was showing either. Connor's eyesight wasn't good enough to make his mickey out, when he turned to the side but, or even right round, the dark hair was unmistakable.

UN-mistakable.

Why didn't the youngfella have a shower-curtain like everyone else if he wanted the window open cos of condensation or whatever? Connor could've understood that, now.

Right, he was going to sit here and watch and see what else he got up to.

Connor couldn't credit it: your man was standing there just, turning this way, then that. After a while, a blue towel flashed around in the gap. Next, the youngfella started to shave or something, to inspect his neck anyway, at what was probably a wash-hand basin on the wall at the window. Then he disappeared altogether. He turned up almost immediately in the room next door but. When he did, it was obvious the towel was round his shoulders and down his back, even though the bedroom window was up as high as the other one but, he came right over and Connor caught an eyeful. He turned away quick, pretended to be looking for Radio Eireann on his son's ghettoblaster.

Connor could now see him in Brendan's mirror, on the chest of drawers. He was sitting wi his bare back to the window, Connor could tell from the movements but that he was putting clean underclothing on. He stood up as he pulled on one of them long

127

baggy T-shirts, young Brendan wore them too, just as it was falling down over him but, a weegirl came into the room, came over towards him, pointing at him, and must have caught him on the chest cos he came falling backwards onto the bed at the window, and the next thing, Holy Jesus, she was on top of him. Holy God. Connor fiddled like mad for Radio Eireann. That was one good thing about Paisley: at least you got good reception for Radio Eireann.

He gave up. He'd have to settle for Radio Scotland just. They were in the middle of the classified results. When he dared to look in the mirror again, the weegirl was still on top of him. She was wearing a pink T-shirt and had plenty to fill it wi. Both her arms went straight down at an angle. Connor could imagine her pinning him down on the bed.

The T-shirt came off – the youngfella's, that is. Connor watched her pull it up over his back and then push him down again. Her head went down, maybe to kiss him. Then up again. And down again. He saw quick flashes of them as they rolled along the bed one way, then the other. She made sure she stayed on top, then disappeared.

Reports were coming in from round the country, Connor but was hardly listening. His foot was itching. He removed his shoe and sock and rubbed between his wee toe and the one next to it. The sensation went through him. He was keeping an eye on the mirror. There was nothing to see at the moment. He knew they were still there but. He'd've seen them going away if they had've.

It was a good while before your woman sat up again. She was still wearing the T-shirt. Holy God, plenty happening, and she still hadn't taken it off for the youngfella. Someone turned up at the toilet next door and stood at it, even though it seemed to be another weegirl.

Connor was rubbing away at his foot. He'd be drawing blood if he didn't watch. Just as the phone-in started, your woman began to bob up and down. She took her top off, showing herself off to the street like that. Connor watched. This was what happened when they didn't have one ounce of religion in them. Her breasts dropped as she struggled to get the top over her head, then she leant down and fell away. Your man half-stood up and you saw the boxers coming down, then he turned and dropped onto her. You saw maybe her knees, but definitely the cheeks of his backside popping up and down above the white of the window ledge. Without stopping, the boy tried to drag the curtain shut, a red triangle swept across to sort-of half-fill the window, another hand but from down below was just as quick and whipped it straight back. They were rolling and tumbling, rolling and tumbling, in the sunlight, the breeze. The answers to questions about the Celtic board, meanwhile, were getting nowhere, slowly.

It was the youngfella who was now in control. His head shot up and there was a knock at the door. Shit in hell. Connor had expected them to buzz him up through the entry system. The sharp knock was repeated. Flip bloody sake. 'Coming!' he shouted. 'It's okay, I'm coming!' He flicked the switch on the radio off and attempted to get back into his shoe and sock, it wasn't succeeding but. He smoothed the duvet, closed the door behind him, and got his backside to the flat door quick.

The telly was still on in the livingroom. He'd pretend he'd dozed off.

It wasn't them. It was a woman, – good-looking, too! 'Oh – you must be Brendan's father!' she said. 'He's your mirror image. Here, the postman left this downstairs with me for him.'

Connor slipped back into the bedroom. When he looked out,

across, full frontals were jumping into their clothes again. It looked like they couldn't do it quick enough.

When the others got back, nothing was said. There was no reason for anything *to be said*, Connor kept reminding himself. He was glad once they were in the car and on their way home but.

Days later, his son phoned the house. When Bernie answered, all he said was 'Hi, is my Da in?' Bernie thought it strange at the time. When Connor went to the phone, 'What? It's me he wants?', Brendan asked him what the hell he'd been doing in his bedroom listening to Radio Scotland? When Connor denied it, 'I swear to God, son, and I wouldn't tell you a lie now', his son just went like that: 'Who the hell was it then? Mr Nobody? It wasn't me, like,' and hung up.

'QUICK! Where's our Dermot? The army's lifted Colum Curran!'

It was his Aunt Bernadette, rushing in.

'Oh – yes, Bridget, yes, Liam, Wee Liam, son!' she said when she saw them.

'Yes, Bernadette!'

His mum stood up to kiss her. She nudged his da to put down his mug to do the same, but Bernadette disappeared out of the room as suddenly as she'd turned up. Liam couldn't get the words out quick enough to tell her Dermot was in the kitchen – she found him first.

'Dermot, quick! Gone run up the street and tell Mrs Curran her Colum's been lifted down the Strand. Tell her I saw it happening on my way home. They've probably only taken him in for questioning, but she wants to get somebody down to the barracks quick.'

Dermot came running out of the kitchen, pulling on his parka. He headed out the door. Bernadette came back in and went over to hug Liam's mum and da. 'You're looking well, sister, dear,' his da said. She was still up to high doh about Colum Curran but.

'Aw God, I could never've imagined thon youngfella getting lifted. He wouldn't do nothing to nobody, ye know. D'yous remember him? Yous must do, sure he was the year below you at the College, Liam, and mind he used to be going steady with Hughie's Patricia's sister, Anna – Anna McGoldrick? Surely to God yous remember him – Colum Curran? He's wild good to my Mammy

131

too, ye know, where is she anyway? Did she go over to the chapel today an' all? Honest to God, I wish she'd lift a hand to help me instead of all the praying she does. I'm the one out working – and I have to come in and do it all. Anyway, I was saying: Colum Curran, he drives my mother everywhere when I'm not here, to the bingo and that. Here, that's an idea: maybe I should get our Eileen to go down to the barracks and put in a word for him. She knows them all, ye know, what wi her running the buses an' all. They might just listen to her. Anyway,' she said, finally sitting down, 'had yous a good journey over? '

'Aye, thanks.'

'Where's the weans all?'

'Out the back, playing.'

'Aye, well just as well they're not out the front ruining my flower beds. I only done them yesterday.'

'There she is now!'

'Where?'

'At the window!'

Bernadette came out. 'Yes, weans! Nice to see yous. I hope yous aren't ruining the grass I did yesterday now?'

She hugged those that went running up to her.

'And what about my goddaughter like? Ciara! Are you not giving your Aunt Bernadette a hug?'

Ciara went over and put her arms round her.

'You might look as if you mean it, weegirl!'

'What are we getting for the tea, Aunt Bernie?' Liam asked to change the subject.

'God's sake, weeboy, I'm only in the door. Let me catch my breath first. Anyway, there's no tea going on until I've seen ma programmes. And your Granny'll want to see the *Ulster News* an' all.'

'Are we getting Derry mince, Auntie Bernie?'

'Maybe, we'll see. Yous'll be getting buck all if you don't give me peace to watch my programme.'

'It's all right. We like *Crossroads* too, Aunt Bernie.'

'It's far too good a night but for weans like you to be inside watching TV. Yous are fine where yous are: outside, playing.' She turned to go back in. 'Mind now, and let me see my programme.'

There was shooting during *Crossroads*. The weans came running in.

'Mum, there's shooting out the front, and Mum – you can hear it!'

'Bad boys are throwing stones, Mum.'

'And bottles too, Dad!'

'Mum, I'm scared, Mum!'

'WEANS!!' It was Bernadette cracking up. 'Now look: I warned yous. I told yous before the programme started I wanted peace to see it. Liam! Talk to them weans of yours, will ye?'

'For God's sake, Bernadette, they're frightened. Give them a chance. They'll calm down in a minute.'

'Well I've not got a minute! There's nothing to be scared of, anyway. It's only shooting. It'll pass – ' Suddenly Bernadette was up out of her seat and roaring out of her but: 'Hey, youngfella! AYE, you, WEEBOY, them there's my flowers. Get away from them or I'm coming out to hit ye a thump! Aye, YOU! I'm warning ye!'

She sat down again.

'Right, weans, come on. Sit down and be quiet,' their da said, looking at her. 'Yous'll be okay. And your Aunt Bernadette wants to see her programme in peace.'

'Sean, get back from the window, son,' their mum said. 'Liam, tell that boy to get back from the window!'

Sean laughed. 'A bottle's after going in the hole at the top of the saracen!'

Ciara jumped up. 'Let me see. I want to see, too!'

'WEANS, sit DOWN! Come on, I'm not telling yous again,' their da said. 'Sit down and behave yourselves – or d'yous want the soldiers coming in to get ye? Cos that's what'll happen, ye know!'

The weans sat down. Their mother went over to keep the youngest ones quiet for Bernadette to see her programme. Annette had started bubbling when her father mentioned the soldiers coming in. Bridget tried to comfort her. 'Shoosh, there's a good girl. Shoosh, everything's going to be okay, shoosh, there's a good girl. That's right: sure there's no need to wor – ' She stopped. She'd seen something. 'Oh Holy God, Liam, Bernadette,' she said. 'There's your mother coming walking back from the chapel, in the middle of all that rioting!'

Bernadette shrugged it off. 'It's all right, she's used to it,' she said. 'And it's not as if they're going to fire at her, is it?'

Liam's mum looked at his da. Part of her wanted to send him

out, part of her definitely didn't. She could tell by looking at him he was in two minds an' all. As he stood up to go out, Bernadette said, 'Where are you off to? Sit down on your backside, you, and just watch her. She'll be giving out stick to them youngfellas in a minute so she will'.

They watched. Sure enough she did. It looked almost comical, right enough.

'I don't know what this street's coming to,' she said as she came in. 'I've told them but: I'm not standing for it, me – Oh: yes, weans! Yes, Bridget, Liam, son!' She hugged and kissed them all, making a great fuss of the weans.

'Had yous a good sailing? Yous must've made good time, I wasn't expecting yous till after. I hope you weren't speeding now, Liam?'

They were stuck in the middle of their tea when the phone rang.

'That was Colum Curran to say he's been released,' Bernadette said when she came back in. 'They didn't do nothing to him.'

'Did ye not know? I could've told ye that!' her mother said. 'Sure Kathleen Curran was arriving to say a prayer of thanksgiving just as I was leaving the chapel. I'd've told ye if I'd thought ye were interested – '

'It's just I saw him getting lifted down the Strand on my way home,' said Bernadette.

'Did ye now?'

'Aye, and I sent our Dermot up the street to tell his mother when I got in – '

'Did ye now? What for, like?'

'Just to let the woman know what was happening to her son.'

'Right, well listen, Bernadette: I told you before. I don't want you running to people when there's trouble with the army. I've told you before: I don't want them at my door – and this is still my house whether you like it or not.'

'She was only trying to help, mother, sure,' Liam's da said.

'Keep out of it, you! You don't know what goes on here. You might think ye do, you don't know the half of it but.' She turned back to the table. 'Eat up, weans! Are yous enjoying your dinner?'

'Uh-huh.'

'Uh-huh? What on under God does that mean? Are yous wee donkeys or something?'

'It means *yes* over in Scotland, Gran,' said Ciara.

'Does it now? Well not in my house it doesn't. Yous'll speak properly here. It's not *uh-huh*, it's *aye*. I'll ask yous again: are yous enjoying your dinner?'

'*Aye*, Gran!'

'Good! I'm glad to hear it. Well, eat to your heart's content. It's not the Waterside you're in now, you know.'

That was a reference to their other gran and her comment once about them eating her out of house and home. Liam's mum looked at his da – he wouldn't take his mother on but.

After the tea, Liam slipped upstairs. He didn't want to be around when the pile of spuds was discovered under the table. He couldn't blame the other weans. There was definitely something sickening about them, something blue and watery in the middle. If ye were going to feed them to the dog but, you didn't lacquer them wi brown sauce and ketchup first. That's why the dog had eaten his but not the others but. Holy hell was going to be let loose when Bernadette discovered them.

The potatoes weren't the only reason for him disappearing upstairs, if he was honest with himself. He was feart, for one thing, that something might happen, something to do with the Troubles. He'd sworn the last time they were over he'd never come back, and now his mum and dad had made him. It wasn't just that but. He was browned off wi them all for calling him 'Wee Liam' an' all. He never got this Big Liam/Wee Liam nonsense back in Scotland. There, he was 'Liam', and his da was 'Mr O'Donnell' or 'your daddy' or 'your dad'. As sure as God but: they were no sooner in the door, he'd hardly sat his bum down, for God sake, before the Derry ones were *Wee-Liam*-ing him left, right and centre. He was raging, knew he'd get a thick ear if he let it show but.

To try and just forget them, he took his bag and emptied it onto the bed. He opened an old jotter. It was French Vocab. He wrote in some phrases he'd picked up or been reminded of since he arrived.

Operation Motorman

senior quartermaster

informer

internment

involved

Involved was the worst. It didn't mean anything like that in Scotland. It sounded dangerous.

Ciara came into the room. 'What are you doing?'

'Looking at my jotter.'

'Which one?'

'French.'

Ciara looked at what he'd written. 'That's not French,' she said.

'So?'

'And anyway, the English is supposed to go in the right-hand column.'

When he didn't take her on, she said, 'I've still not told you what I came up to tell ye!'

'What?'

'The soldiers are downstairs!'

Jesus! Liam had known deep down something was going to happen. He'd thought it would be the spuds but.

'It's all right, they're not going to raid us.'

'How not?'

'One of them is Mark Dawson's big brother! Dad says for you to come down to meet him. He recognised Dad soon as he came in,' said Ciara. 'Are ye coming?'

'Suppose I might as well. I hate his brother's guts but.'

'And this is my oldest boy, Liam, named after myself,' his da said when Liam opened the livingroom door. Dawson's big brother was sitting on Gran's settee beside an enormous big black guy and another soldier. Their rifles were on the floor in front of them, between them and the ones that had got up to give them a seat.

Mugs of tea and spring-sprongs and fig rolls were arriving on a tray. 'Come on on in, son. It's okay, they're not going to harm us.'

As Liam stepped over folk to get to the hearth, his da said, 'What do you think – this one's a St Mirren supporter!'

Dawson's brother laughed. The other two grinned, waiting for the funny side to be explained.

'Beat you lot in the Dryburgh Cup anyway,' Liam said.

'Alasdair is a Rangers supporter, son,' his da said, quietly.

Liam wasn't impressed. 'We beat them an' all in our section of the League Cup!'

Alasdair didn't laugh this time. 'Enjoy it while it lasts, son. It'll be a different story once the season starts,' he said. You could see as soon as he'd opened his mouth but, he knew he'd come on too heavy.

There was a silence. It was a rule in their house that if you were going to pick on anyone, you picked on someone your own size. To cover up the awkwardness, the soldiers took a gulp of tea. The bin-lids started just as they were putting their mugs down.

Liam's mother jumped. 'Jesus, Mary and St Joseph!' she said. 'What's that?'

'Somebody getting raided,' Bernadette said, without as much as looking at the soldiers, you could tell it was directed at them but.

'Gran, the women are at your gate, Gran!' said Sean who'd headed straight for the window.

'Holy God, they think I'm being raided!'

Some of the weans laughed. 'It's no laughing matter, you lot.

They think my house is being turned upside down by these boys. Right, lads, OUT! Quick: don't let them see yous were sitting on my settee!'

You could tell Liam's da was wanting something.

'Mother, Bridget and I were thinking of going out after – d'you mind?'

'Were yous now? Well, as long as you don't think I'm babysitting. Yous'll have to ask Bernadette. I'm going to the bingo. It's the big Snowball at the Star tonight.'

His da went into the kitchen to whisper to Bernie. Bernie wouldn't whisper back but. Liam heard her saying: 'Aye, all right, Liam, but I'm telling ye: you shouldn't be going out. They're expecting trouble. Don't tell me you haven't seen the bonfires now. But on ye go: go ahead if you want to.'

Liam's mum put the weans to bed before they went. She'd to throw his da out of the bathroom. The stupid big lump started shaving to go out before the weans had brushed their teeth even. 'Away and put clean underclothing on instead'.

'What for? It's not Christmas!' their da said.

'Very funny! In case there's any bother at the checkpoint.'

'Don't forget to say your prayers now,' Bridget said as she turned the light off and closed the door behind her.

The weans hadn't settled yet: the girls were side-by-side down one double bed, the three boys had a bit more room in the other.

Their mother came back in. 'One other thing, folks,' she said.

'Don't ever let me find good Irish potatoes under your Mammy Donnell's table again. You're lucky your Aunt Bernadette didn't find them: she'd've done her nut. And what if them soldiers had discovered them, ay? They'd've thought your Mammy Donnell was a dirty bitch and that everybody over here was like that.'

Some of the weans laughed cos their mum had said a bad word. She warned them but. She said, 'Never again, okay? Promise?'

'Promise,' a couple of them mumbled.

Liam could've stayed up, he was old enough, he went to bed with the rest of them but. If there was going to be trouble, he'd rather be asleep when it happened. The last time they'd been over, Gran had tried to make out it was fireworks, it was obvious but it was shooting and bombs down the town.

He heard nothing that night, still couldn't get to sleep but. Eventually he realised he was worried about his mum and dad. He wouldn't be able to sleep until they came home, till he knew they were safe.

At twenty past three, they still weren't back yet still. That was when Sean started to stir, Sean, the sleepwalker in the family.

Liam decided to follow him. The sight of Sean at the top of the stairs minded him a bit of *Heidi*. He sneaked down after him, past the two portholes where the stairs went round a corner. That was the bit Liam was scared of: where the army would see you if you put the lights on – and where they'd get suspicious if they spotted you in the dark, creeping round. He hated walking there: he'd already worked out where any bullet would hit you, depending on which stair you were on. Through the ankle on that stair there would be the most painful, he reckoned.

At the bottom of the stairs, Sean flattened the dog, nearly. He didn't wake up but. Liam followed him through the hall, into the kitchen, and out the back door towards the coal shed. He watched as Sean lifted the lid off Gran's bin. He looked like your man wi the gong at the pictures. Suddenly Liam realised what he was goney do. Flip sake, he'd start a bloody riot if he done that at this time of night. As the lid hit the concrete but, a man did a rugby tackle on him and a woman nearly screamed.

surviving uncertain fates 13

At some point I started: jumped awake; my hands darting into the dish on the tray in front of me; the tips of my fingers landing full-square on chicken-skin I hadn't eaten. Drew, when I looked, was still across the aisle. Beyond the exits next to our seats snored folk who'd been to the same island, among them the father of five who'd hung, drunk, over the bannister, toddler-on-his-shoulders an' all, as a slow queue, well past its sleep, worked its way down to the plane. The memory of everyone side-stepping the duty-free dribble from that guy's bag, and I dozed off again.

Some time later came the chime: seat-belts for landing, doors to manual, etc. We both woke this time, turned, and looked at each other. I wasn't with it – said so, myself. Drew nodded, grinned, said, 'Great impersonation of Tommy Cooper earlier, by the way!'

'So you saw that, did ye?'

Chuffed with his ammo for future slaggings, he grinned again.

'Bastard! Never miss a trick, do ye?'

He was on for a carry-on, launched into a Cooper impersonation just as I did. The meal trays had been removed in the meantime.

We landed. The worst winter this century, police saying not to set out unless you have to. We had to. Drew driving, the long trip north from the airport, in the highest gear possible, crawling, concentrating. Ahead of us the likelihood of burst pipes, flats in a pure mess when we got there.

'Just like that!' he quoted again, out-of-the-blue, and laughed. I laughed, too, able to take it, as he ooh-yugh-ed and wiped his fingers clean. Just summit else he'd witnessed, shared, I thought. His laugh, though, faded: eyes now studied me, were watching for reactions.

'Can I tell you something?' he asked.

I hesitated before I nodded, I suppose.

'There's something I should tell you,' he told me.

He took me back to Boxing Day night on Fuerteventura. The shellfish soup, the paella outside the restaurant. I minded fine. Minded, too, the girl who was singing; her sidekick on keyboards, his medley of Eurovision entries.

It was Drew's turn to nod, and I could see he reckoned it safe to continue.

'Well, mate, that night, I woke up, desperate for a slash, and when I came back: way you were lying – shoulda seen it!'

He paused, maybe testing the water.

'Out wi it, ya bastard!' I laughed, like there was nothing I couldn't handle. 'What was it about me, then?'

'Not so much you as the pillow,' he said.

'Pillow?' I asked. Bugger was enjoying this.

'Well, it wasn't so much *across* your bed, as *down* it!'

'Aw naw!' I groaned. 'So I'd been shagging the pillow and you, ya bastard, saw the evidence. Ya jammy – !'

That was the reaction he wanted, of course: revenge for the

time he was paralytic in Stirling and I claimed he'd snogged Susie Fraser.

I was damned if I was saying another word. I wouldn't give him the satis-bloody-faction. He reached across but, and sort-of shook my shoulder. 'It's not what you're thinking,' he said.

'Both hands on the wheel, you!' I barked, shrugging him off. 'Specially in these conditions.'

'But it's nuthin embarrassing, mate,' he protested. 'It's *good*. Speaks for you. That's why I wanted to tell you – '

'Right, that's it! Stop the fuckin car!' I said. 'This'd better be swift 'n' painless – for *your* sake. Pull in at a convenient place and effin out with it, mate!'

'And don't forget your hazards!' I added as he came to a halt. Way I was feeling, he'd be needing them.

What he told me was brilliant.

Seems I was facing the wall, and my sheet was well down the bed, practically off me. Thing he focused on but was the pillow, parallel to my back, behind me: where Claire had been until six months ago, where she'd been since second-year uni.

'So that's what this is about? Us separating?'

'Shoosh,' he said.

It seems my left arm was out from under me and over and round the pillow. 'Round *her*,' as Drew said. 'Round Claire,' he added as I looked at him, no' believing I was hearing this. Ye go on holiday wi the bugger, ten days over Christmas and New Year, and on the last leg of the journey home he starts playing the amateur fuckin psychologist?

'So six months later, I'm still not over it, still missing her. Is that what you're saying?' I asked. 'Me hugging the pillow contradicts everything I told you down by the pool, confided as we hiked across hardened lava. Is that the story? I don't still love her, if that's what you're suggesting.'

'Naw, that's not what I'm saying, mate. It's more than that. What I'm saying is: at that moment, I saw you, and I saw the pillow, and I saw what she walked out on. I saw the love you're capable of giving – and I'm no' goney see that otherwise, am I?' he added hurriedly. Must've seen I wasn't sure how to take this. 'All I'm saying, mate, is: what I saw underlined what I've told you before: you're some guy – '

He reached across and patted my shoulder again; looked me in the eye.

'*Her* loss,' he said.

You'd forgive me for thinking that that was that: that the heavy bit was over, and I could now relax. While he was at it but, he decided to tell me it was as if I slept in slow motion. I looked at him again: the fuck was he on about now?

The explanation could've been worse: before he dropped off again himself, he'd seen me turn in my sleep. Seems I did so fraction-by-fraction, millimetre-by-millimetre. As if someone had been sitting opposite me with the remote-control, pressing the still-frame and slow buttons. 'Aye, like *you*, ya perv!' I tried to protest; there was no stopping him but. At one point, he said, he thought I would reach a brink, then topple over or collapse. Even then but, it seems, I rolled in controlled fashion onto my back.

Seeing me, he'd ended up wondering whether he slept in slow

motion, too? Did everybody? Funny how he'd never noticed with Sandra or Ann or Marie, he said. Or with Clare, *his* Clare, he hastened to add, Clare-without-an-I, or Valerie or Sam, for that matter. He'd got onto Naomi, Pamela and Sharon before he couldn't keep a straight face any more. I hit him a thump. 'Braggin proddy cunt!' I said.

'Least I've got summit to brag about!' he'd answer, I thought. What he actually said was: 'Maybe you've got to be on the other side of the room from someone, sometimes, to see what's going on.'

What *really* tickled the bugger but was: before he conked out again himself, he'd spotted that my right hand had a hold of the last corner of the sheet, and always, always, no matter what way I turned, made sure my privates were covered. The distance between the sheet and my stomach remained *constant*, he maintained; the *precision* was incredible.

'So there ye go: virginity well oot the windae – still the bashful Tim but!' he teased.

'Least I wisni playin wi myself like you'd've been,' I joked. 'Naw, that's the magnetic pull of the Catholic belly-button! Makes sure we stay *dacent*. You Prods haveni got that!'

There was a pause. Him (unusually) not rising to the bait. Me realising *that*, and *why*, my hold of the sheet had been perfected while I was still under my mother and father's roof. Minding being lucky as fuck the morning my da came in (something he never did) to say John Paul I was dead. Sometimes things crop up that make you see you're not as free as you think. – Claire and her convent-girl night-shirt came to mind an' all; Claire who made out she was being *subjected to eyefuls* if ever I slept naked beside her. Claire

147

who accepted nudity only in the bathroom or when *doing it*. If she wasn't up for it, she didn't want to have *that bloody thing* staring her in the face, she said.

Drew broke the silence, could sense something was wrong.

'Did I do right to tell you, mate?' he asked. 'Bout the pillow and that?'

'Aye, mate. Cheers. Ye did.'

I was lucky he'd seen me. Lucky he'd decided to tell me. I'd tell him another time about Claire; nuthin he doesn't know, anyway. Would have to give him a laugh an' all: tell him about JP1 dying – and me starkers and hardly under the bloody duvet.

Right now but, I wanted to savour what he'd told me. *The love you're capable of giving*. Was the same boy said I always *pull sooner than I surrender* (that's the Catholic in me, too, he claims). And when I was doing my *hurt-hedgehog impersonations* (as he called them) after losing Claire, was him coaxed me into opening up again; who insisted that *having nobody is not nothing*.

I'd been quiet for too long. Was his turn to feel nervous.

'Did I, mate?' he pressed. 'Are ye sure? Did I do right to tell ye?'

I looked at him. 'Aye, mate, nay worries, ye did right. Ta.'

I waited until I saw him relax, then hit him wi 'Last fuckin time I share a room wi you but, ya poof!'

He laughed. We shook on it. A clumsy attempt at giving each other five. He studied my face, grinned, made to get into gear; interrupted himself but to look at me again and give me a hug.

'Cheers, mate,' I muttered as I eased out of it.

He checked his blind spot and we set off again.

stranraer-larne-derry 14
(for the third time)

Liam's heart was in his stomach an' any minute now, his stomach was going to come flying out of his mouth. It wouldn't be touching the sides when it did. His da was putting the foot down to try and make the boat, and it was as if every curve on the road was bowling through the youngfella while it was at it. The rocks and the water's edge on one side, roadside walls whizzing past on the other, didn't help. The worst thing but was: every time Liam thought the worst of it was behind him, his da hammered into another bloody bend. Ardwell-Lendalfoot-Ballantrae had him turning God knows what colours. Low Kilpin, High Kilpin, an' he was very nearly pukin. He wouldn't like to be his mother in front of him if he did.

Poor youngfella: if you'd asked beforehand, it wouldn't've been bringing his eggs & toast back up he'd've been worried about, but crapping his pants. He'd filled his nappy grand-style, sure, when his mother and father first mentioned *heading over home* for the summer. He hadn't been the only one either. When he said to Ciara and Annette, they admitted they were shitting themselves too. The thing about Paisley was: you got used to not having stones and bottles flying, soldiers patrolling the streets, again. And when it wasn't happening round about you, when you didn't have Mammy Donnell to put her arm round you and hold you and tell you it was okay, that everything would be all right, you got afraid of the rioting again, even if, the summer before, it had ended up not bothering you.

In the run-up to going this time, Liam and Annette and Ciara talked non-stop about Derry. The more they talked, the worse their visions of checkpoints and barricades got; not to mention bomb-scares and shootings. The Wee Ones caught wind of this and they got jumpy too. In the end, they all ended up so buckin terrified, Liam led the delegation to go and tell their mum. Bridget managed to calm them down but, to persuade them it was alright. Their daddy had been on the phone, she said, and everyone in Ireland said things had quietened down, there was nothing to worry about.

'You alright there, Liam?'

It was his mum – worried he was being so quiet, maybe.

'Aye, I'm fine – '

He didn't want to speak too soon – it felt like his stomach was settling but. He joined in singing *Oh – I'm going to Barbados* even, when, finally, they spotted the boat. The rest of them had been singing it since Paisley, wi Annette impersonating the pilot speaking. Liam could've hung them bloody up, he'd been too angry to open his mouth but.

'MADE IT!!!' their da roared, pulling into the SEA-LINK car-park. The weans all cheered. Rear doors flew open and the weans were jumping out even as their da was doing handbrake and neutral.

Liam sat where he was for a minute, enjoying the fresh air. It was great not having weans digging into him any more. He could see there wasn't one of them wasn't looking forward to Derry now, looking forward to their aunts and uncles, thon kind of thing. It would be okay if you got to go to Donegal or Galway, he told himself. The trick was to get yourself invited. He himself was likely to join Paddy and Fiona and their lot in Buncrana. Maureen had said on the phone that whoever wanted to could go to Malin Head but they would have to take turns cos she was short of space. Gran and Aunt Bernie had already promised to take Ciara and Annette to Knock (Ciara was Gran's favourite, and her and Annette were like twins). They'd maybe even head Down South while they were at it.

'Right! Back into the car!' their da shouted. It was time to drive on.

The car jolted onto the ramp.

'This is it,' Liam thought, into himself. 'No turning back!'

If he was honest, there were things, nothing-to-do-with-the-Troubles things, he was still dreading. The instant heat-spots, for a start. 'God, look, so they are! They're out in hives, Bridget – look!' Gran would say. They'd hardly set foot in the place before they always came out in them. 'It's the change of air,' their mother would say. 'Well, it's certainly not the bedclothes. I've checked the bed-clothes,' Gran would answer. Bottles and bottles of *Carmoline Lotion* they'd go through, trying to get rid of them.

The potatoes were disgusting an' all, Ciara reminded him, as Liam led them up to the deck. He'd promised his mother to look after them all, *each and every one of them*, if she let them go. His mother wasn't to know what he knew: that the Orangemen who'd been over in Glasgow for the Big March were already up there, puking. Boking their guts over the side, they were. 'There but for the Grace of God – ' (as Gran would've said), Liam thought when he saw them.

He couldn't resist letting the weans watch. It was a brilliant laugh an' they pure gutted themselves when some man muttered, 'That's a strange way to feed the sea-gulls!' Wee Sean couldn't get over the fact that the one with hair had eaten cabbage. 'Him there' he kept saying, 'him with the black hair: it's white cabbage he's throwing up!'

Eventually, the fascination wore off, and it was time to get down to business. The Big Ones had promised – *pwomised*, Cahal kept reminding them – to tell the Wee Ones what to watch out for in Derry. They wanted to warn them – now they were out of ear-shot – about the bad points, and to fill them in on what to do. The Wee Ones were too young to mind, themselves, from the last time.

The moment had come. They'd to sit down nice first but, Ciara insisted. The weans parked their bums. Liam organised them into a horseshoe. He rolled his sleeves up, even, the way he saw his da doing. In no time at all, you wouldn't've got a word in: one idea was triggering off the next; one memory bringing back others. There was one thing they all agreed on but: *definitely* the worst thing about Derry was that Gran and Bernie *scraped* the potatoes – and didn't *peel* them like Mum.

'Even if you put Heinz Ketchup on, or Daddy's Red Sauce, it's disgusting,' Liam said. 'When you bite into them, it's like there's a skin between the red sauce and the inside of the potato.'

'Aye,' said Ciara, 'and if you cut them open, there's something kinda bluey and watery in the middle, and that's what makes them really horrible.'

'Ciara's right,' Annette added, 'and the last time we were always letting on to be sick. We took it in turns to run to the toilet. Then, after a while, we'd come back and say, "I'm sorry, Auntie Bernie, but I can't eat my dinner tonight. My stomach's bothering me." And you wouldn't have to eat it!'

The Wee Ones were killing themselves. Liam spotted Ciara looking round everyone and liking the fact they were having a good laugh together, that noone was fighting. Ciara was the kinda person that mattered to.

'It was a sin before God so it was,' Annette continued. 'You want to have seen the number of potatoes they were throwing out!'

'Good Irish spuds,' Ciara said. That was a quotation.

'It was really disgusting but,' Liam confirmed. 'Even if you lacquered them wi brown sauce, you couldn't eat them.'

Ciara laughed. 'Aye! D'you mind the first night the last time? We all tried to feed them to the dog, slipping them under the table.' She stood up to impersonate it. 'Here, boy! There's a nice potato for you, there's a good boy.' The others laughed. They could see the invisible potato remained in Ciara's hand, that the dog wasn't taking it. 'What's wrong? D'ye not like it, Shep?' Ciara went on. 'But *Shep*, it's lovely, Shep! Here, boy. That's right, don't bother wi his oul potato. C'm'on over here an' take mine. Mine's nicer. There's a good dog. SHEP!! Would ye take the buckin thing, ye big brute ye!'

Ciara stopped. The others were sore laughing. She could see it.

'That wasn't all but,' said Liam, laughing, 'then George Dunlop came in, Bernie's boyfriend, and there was about fifteen big boiled potatoes under the table, and George looked down and said, "Naw, weans, don't be doing that, now. Sure Shep doesn't lik brown sauce". No kiddin ye, that's what he said!'

By this time, they were rolling about the deck, helpless. Folk were looking at them, wondering what the joke was. One woman was shaking her head.

'Aye, but the really disgustin thing,' Annette said, 'was when Uncle Dermot came home in the evening, and his dinner would be in the oven, and Gran or Aunt Bernie would've put a plate over it. And when Dermot lifted the top plate off, some of the potato would come away wi it, and the gravy would be all dried in, all dark brown or even black, and the peas would be all shrivelled up, and Dermot would sit down and actually eat it!!'

'Aw, shut up, you. You'll have me throwin up in a minute!'

Liam was the only one to mind Aunt Roisin trying to cut a family-sized block of Neapolitan ice-cream wi an old bread knife on the wee shelf at the front of the sink – and the ice-cream falling into the dishwater. And her fishing it out and serving it anyway.

'You're making that up!' Ciara protested.

'Naw I'm not. Honest. And she didn't even rinse it, honest to God she didn't – and it was like: dirty dishwater all over the pink and the yellow and the brown.'

'Aw, shut up! You're disgustin so ye are!'

Liam's story minded Annette of the time Roisin dropped cigarette ash in the trifle she was making and just lifted it out wi a tea-spoon. The weans told her to shut up but: their stomachs were turning, they couldn't take any more. Just at that moment, the announcement came, anyway, for car passengers to return to their vehicles.

They hardly saw a soldier hardly between the boat and Derry. The Derry ones had been right enough in what they'd said on the phone. Looking out the window as you drove through, you didn't get the impression any more that shooting and rioting could break out any minute. Or that a bomb could go off.

They arrived safe. It felt odd going into the house, even though it was their gran's and they'd been before. There was new wallpaper in the livingroom again. The furniture was in the same place but. Plus: the smells were the same. It was only in their gran's house you got them smells. She tended to overdo it wi the Domestos.

It was time for the *Ulster News*, nearly. When she was done hugging them, their gran sat down beside the fireplace again. Even when she was watching TV, Liam noticed, she was all the time keeping an eye on the street.

'You don't get as many foot-patrols these days, praise the Lord,' she said, shifting from one hip to the other, and pulling down her pinafore.

'Aye, it's some difference, Mums,' their mum answered.

Apart from Liam who was in the armchair at the window and getting a creak in his neck, the weans were lined up along the settee. The row of different-coloured sandals and wee white ankle-socks looked comical. The weans, for once in their lives, weren't saying nothing. It wasn't like them at all, the O'Donnell brigade wasn't saying nothing but.

'What's wrong wi yis all? Have yis lost your tongues, or something?' their gran asked. She sounded offended. It wasn't as if she was full of bars but herself: apart from the shooting up the street the night before, and the man next door suddenly taking a heart-attack and leaving behind a wife and seven weans ('Thirty-four years of age, he was. Terrible shook up, she is.'), there wasn't that much happening.

'They're probably just tired after the journey, Mums', Bridget said, to try to appease her.

Bridget was wondering where the buck that husband of hers was. The big so-and-so had disappeared out the door as soon as they got in – and it obviously wasn't to park the car as she'd thought. Wasn't as if Dermot and him were bringing the stuff in either. Bernie was taking her bloody time coming home, an' all.

When Bernie got in, she put Derry Mince and Derry Sausages on for the tea. The weans praised the Lord: avoiding the dreaded spuds, they were.

The next morning, even so, they were all out in hives again, and by the evening, a strange tummy-bug was going round. Their mother put it down to the Derry air. 'Your arse in parsley!' their gran, when she heard her, said – no way was she goney have a word said against her home town. 'Yis must've brought it wi yis. Don't gi'e's that! Derry didn't do thon to yis that quick!'

world enough, and time 15

Up to high doh, Mick McGlinchey was, 'n' sweatin buckets, as he crashed his way up the now movin'*Ferdinand Raimund*, the 18.17 from Vienna to Graz. His heart or his back: he didn't know which was breakin most. It wasn't so much the rucksack as his shitin fuckin case – handle had the hands burnt off him as he *huff* steered the *puff* thing with his right *huff* fuckin knee. His *Kreislauf* was pounding, his coordination crap. Didn't help, of course, that he was cursin himself: fact he never bloody learned. He was always the same, sure: arrivin as his effin train was leavin.

Folk, to make things worse, were showin no consideration. Time and time again, things would grind to a halt. Some cunt in his *Lederhose*'d be getting out his paper, or puttin his hat on the rack, say. Or some wee wean would be cutey-cuteyin, or goin all-shy on some auld dear. That's right, folks, ignore me just! *Ignore* my case, the queue o crabbit buggers stuck behind me! Worse still were the Smoking bits. Wouldn't be long before the bog-awful imports would have him explodin.

So fuckin much for 'total fuckin pro'.

So fuckin much for 'in control'.

373:66

        373:66

                373:66

wasn't gettin any closer. Not when the carriages changed from aircraft-style to the old compartments, even: the six-seaters. He was meltin now, Mick, beneath his coat, though he'd undone his buttons 'n' it was minus-whatever outside. Twenty-eight kilos in his case felt more like bastarn forty. Still, he battled on. Past folk without seats, perched on the fold-down ones. Past folk who'd booked Non-Smoking – only to chain-smoke outside their shitin compartments. Past predominantly Slavs. That was the thing about this part of Austria, Mick knew from previous trips. Forget Julie Andrews. Soon as you set foot in VIENNA (SOUTH), ye were leavin Europe as ye knew it. Kick in the arse you were now, sure, from Zagreb or Sarajevo.

His compartment, when he got there, was unexpectedly plush: silvery upholstery; posh white covers on the head-rests. Three of the six seats were taken – bummer!. He wasn't in the mood for company, he wasn't. Had hoped it would be empty.

One look was enough: these'uns were Austrian, alright. They were a recognisable type. A type he, at least, recognised. Young, 'with it'. Strangely *formal*, business-like but. Naw a bundle of laughs, exactly. Ye wouldn't get that at home: way they barely even acknowledged each other. Be that as it may: MiseryGuts at the windae there would have to shift his stuff.

373:66 – A ye, that's what it says.

Mick checked his ticket against the panel at the entrance. Four reserved: the two at the window, two at the aisle. Turns out MiseryGuts had parked himself on 66; was usin his own as a table. Mick's heart sank. Mood he was in, he knew not to open his mouth – or he'd bite the bastard's head off.

'Grüss Gott,' he muttered as he slid open the door and headed into the middle.

'Grüss Gott,' responded the Austrians, hardly lookin.

Women's man as ever, he'd sit beside Gudrun here. No between SeatPincher and the other guy. He got his rucksack off 'n' onto the rack – book he was readin could wait – then went back into the corridor to fetch his case. Knowin his luck, the trolley would be right along if he tried to leave it.

Two Austrian guys looked worried as he inched his way in. Don't move to help, anyone, now! Two square feet he had (if that), to play wi. Were they afraid he was goney do them an injury? Afraid he was goney flatten them? Back home, by now, someone would've offered him a hand. Or he could've turned to someone 'n' given it: 'Could ye gi'e's a hand, mate?' No here but. He took a deep breath. McGlinchey was fit for them. HERE-I-COME-READY-OR-NOT!! *Darf ich?* he went, 'n' they'd to shift their feet as he slipped his case beneath them. Pity he couldn't photograph the looks he got. Obviously didn't think it would go, the cunts. He knew it *would* but. Long as it wasn't bulgin. See? The girl, at least, smiled.

He shed his overcoat, kept his jacket on but. Wanted to cool down afore exposing his armpits. He wobbled a bit as he stepped back out: Nearly had me in your lap, Gudrun, love! Sub-zero or not, he opened the windae. Great to breathe freely, it was. Deep breaths would calm him. Stop him sweatin like a fuckin cart-horse. Only then would he re-join his *microcosm*.

He knew who he wished he was joinin –

Her in the sauna last night: sprawled out on the marble; the wavy fuckin locks, straight out of Klimt.

Vienna passed in the dark.

Man fährt wieder Bahn – The slogan summed his week up. *Doing it by train. Again.* MEIDLING had already been. NEUSTADT or MÜRZ-ZUSCHLAG, maybe even, was next. He loved the sound o that: MÜRZ-ZU-SCHLAG. Least he hadn't to change in buckin BRUCK. He couldn't've faced it.

Naw, he could take a deep breath, relax, take some time to himself, *enjoy* the trip, instead. Was a job well done, after all! He couldn't wait to see Baker's coupon when he presented them all wi the figures! McGlinchey triumphs again! Targets exceeded, ya bass! December was another month when he'd take every bonus goin. The ten days in Tunisia, say. The weekend in Prague.

Pity it was so dark, getting. Scenery up ahead was spectacular. If only ye'd time to spend in it! Was the scenery that attracted him, the scenery that stopped him from delegating. Despite the early starts; the long fuckin hauls to reach each subsequent client. The work, of course, would've *flown* him. He refused point-blank but. 'No way! I'd be up and down lik a yoyo!' Credit where credit's due: for once, they hadn't pushed it.

The same route for years, he'd been doing. From Zurich, he headed to Innsbruck. From there, across to Vienna. Vienna, down to Graz. Then back up the middle to Linz. From there, via Salzburg, to Munich. The mountains in the middle slowed things down. Was stunnin if you got the weather but. A case of jigsaw-lid after jigsaw-lid, as your man had said on the wireless.

Austria: he'd known fuck-all about the place, had asked to be shifted but, when Deutschland started to bore him. German was spoken in Austria, too. There was a whole culture but, a *different* culture, that could maybe appeal to him maybe. He'd hoped so, anyway. If not, was time to fuckin chuck it.

Eff-all was what he'd known, right enough:

> Archduke Franz Ferdinand & Hitler
>
> Julie Andrews & *The Sound of Music*
>
> Falco & Schwarzenegger

was as far as it fuckin went, about. Oh – 'n' the fact it was '*chiefly Roman Catholic*'. Hair on the back of his neck rose, always, when anyone specified *Roman*. A sign to keep your wits about ye, it was. Back then, anyway. Back then, as an undergrad, listenin to the Prof, he'd wondered, Mick, how the same boy viewed *Irish* Catholics. He'd survived but. Got through okay. Had put his head down just 'n' worked his butt off, steerin clear of the Luther option.

Aye, Austria was Catholic, alright! Wi some helluva dodgy bishops, if you believed the papers. Last time he was here, there'd been *allegations*. About the Pope's favourite cardinal, it was, 'n' young boys. Some punter'd come out wi stuff, many, many years on. Same back home, of course. Only puzzlin thing was: why nothing was done sooner. People had *known*, sure. Same wi priests 'n' women: people *knew*. Before the *Thorn Birds*, even. He'd heard stuff himself as a wean. So why'd there no been stronger protests sooner?

He fished out a chewing-gum to clear the taste in his mouth.

Last night's dream, christ!

He'd forgot all about it. Now but, it was back 'n' clear as a bell. Him in the showers, wi a hard-on up to his shoulder (aye, in yir dreams, Mick!), tight against the wall to conceal it. Folk behind him. Then, in a room, in some kind-of hostel; foreign; no even his room even; him clothed, on top o the bed, 'n' a girl comes in, 'n' at first he resists cos he knows the guy whose room it is – to see, anyway – 'n' knows he's about; then but, he surrenders though he's no protection, 'n' she sucks him off just about 'n' lo 'n' behold: another one comes in – gorgeous, this time – 'n' sits on him 'n' he comes right away nearly, knowin *This could be the death of me*; he's still hard but, -ish, 'n' stays in, shovin, much as he can anyway, *pressin* for all he's worth, the knuckles in her mouth bit off him.

Other three had forgotten him by the time he went back in. Girl was the most pleasant: wasn't afraid of her face crackin. He picked up on her perfume as he sat down. Nice! Still no looker but. Student-type, cropped hair, not a pick on her. This was what ye got: if it wasn't the monied middle-aged type, the totally stylised type, this was what ye got in terms of Austrian women. Widni be invitin her to Glasgow if they did start talkin.

The two guys looked smug bampots. Quick glance was all he needed to suss MiseryGuts, there. SeatPincher was the anaemic vegan Christian type. Passionate wasn't a word he understood. Sittin like a buckin monk, the boy was. Hunched o'er his missal. Not that the other guy was any better! Looked the ac-tor type, he did. Like the asshole Fiona went out wi afore him. Mick feigned interest in the landscape, was studyin the boy's reflection but. *Lanky*, above all, he was. Long face. Black hair, thinnin on top. Bit of a poser, in his polo neck, trousers 'n' black patent shoes. Lik Bruno Ganz, a bit; or him in *Mephisto*. This boy'd a book in his hands, too. Was givin nothin away, way he was holdin it.

Mick rose to get his own book. Unpacked some food while he was at it. Soon as he sat down again, he knew he couldn't read. No the way his head was, he couldn't. He piled his things beside the stick insect's – who smiled: Christ! A *smile*! He could nod off any minute, it felt like, so – no wantin to slabber on Gudrun, like – he leant on the arm-rest where his things were.

He came to a couple of times. Checked where he was; what the others were up to; dozed off again. Way his head was against his coat, nae cunt could get at his wallets. Third time he woke, the stick insect was leavin. Other two were polite back. Mick grabbed the chance to shift his stuff. Park my arse where The Wristless Wonder should've been, 'n' wi a bit of luck, nobody'll want my seat. Girl smiled her approval, stretched, made herself comfy too.

Female shoes, feet.

Way the shoes *gloved* her feet.

Lecker.

Die Fahrkarten, bitte. Billets, s'il vous plaît. Tickets, please!

Ticket collector 'n' his wee spiel dragged Mick out of his sleep. A proper sleep, too. Girl, it turned out, was preparin to leave. Ticket collector satisfied himself 'n' off she went.

'*Wiederschaun.*'

'*Wiederschaun.*'

'*Und frohes Fest!*'

She was right enough, christ! Christmas was days away only.

He handed over his book of tickets, issued from London. Ticket collector insisted on goin through them. Ages passed before, finally, he punched a couple.

Actor seemed to clock the document wallet as it was handed back.

He realises you're not Austrian. *Shit*

Pretend to read or summit. Last thing you want's a conversation.

Mick opened his book where he'd left off. A few phrases, and it all came floodin back: Moira & Roddy. Moira makin pizza, Roddy – door snibbed – runnin a bath. Him: home to go out again. Her: heart on her sleeve. Tryin. Later: her on her own-y-o, all woman on the floor. Stretch-in. Yo-ga. He'd ended up wi a hard-on, Mick, first time he read this. No this time but. Oh, 'n' aye: the cop at the windae –

Would he get tae partake of her pizza? Tae gi'e her one?

Mick laughed into himself – minded o the one about the blond who goes up to the bar 'n' asks for a double entendre. He could still see Gavin, Peter 'n' Wee Duncan slammin their pints down 'n' pissin themselves, first time that one was told. Three o them in their striped shirts, ties undone, sleeves rolled up to show their Rolexes off, slammin their pints down 'n' repeatin the punchline.*So he gave her one!!* Ye could count on Wee Duncan to repeat it once too often. *So he* – To leave it soundin flat.

JESUS FUCK!

The ac-tor, Mick now noticed, had slipped into the lotus position – his shoes magically beneath his seat; his long skinny feet in thin socks, flexin, wrigglin, breathin. Austrians seemed no to have a problem wi socks 'n' feet. Mick did. Odour or no odour, he didni want subjected.

He forced himself to concentrate on what he was readin instead. Was aware of himself soon grinnin.

Funny.

Funny but no funny.

Wincin at times, too.

It had to happen: just as he reached the final furlong, the Austrian asked what his book was? Shit. Like being mid-shag, it was, 'n' the phone goin.

Least he'd asked in German. Hadn't spotted the documents, maybe.

Mick held up his book. Present from Fiona, for some reason, while they were together still. *Where you find it* meant bugger all to Mr Ganz, obviously. *Wo du sie findest*, Mick said in German for him. Mindin suddenly that 'it' referred to 'love' – Janice had mentioned the song at the reading – he spelt it out: 'Also: Wo du *Liebe* findest'.

Boy took the book, studied the design – two bits of loveheart-shaped toast; piece below the title wi a bite taken out – then turned to the back cover. Mick couldn't mind what the blurb said. Minded the ham sandwich just. Heart-shaped again. Enormous.

'*Zeitgenössische schottische Literatur,*' he explained.

'*Studieren Sie Englisch?*' the guy asked – takin Mick for a student.

'*Nein, ich komme aus Schottland!*'

Guy didn't comment on his German. He nodded – in recognition, presumably, just. '*Wie James MacMillan!*' he gave it next.

Mick agreed, eagerly. '*Ja, ja! Genau!*'

'Jimmy's music's great!' he added.

'Jimmy?' the Austrian asked.

'Yeah, Jimmy!' Mick confirmed. 'Back home, we know our artists – '

Again, it sounded odd; formal. Was partly the fact ye had to explain; partly the fact he'd pronounced it so clearly.

'Or feel as if we do – ' Fiona did, anyhow.

He still wisni happy. Needed another go. *'Kultur ist in Schottland hands-on,'* he announced next.

The Austrian laughed. Even moreso when Mick added: *'Hands-on-er als in Deutschland oder Österreich.'*

Guy was starin ahead, now. Was tryin – maybe – to imagine that in Austria.

'Und das ist die Janice!' Mick said, beginnin to wonder when he'd get his book back.

The guy grinned, held it up. *'Ein Jennice!'* he declared.

Ye could see he was full of the idea as he handed Mick it back.

'Und was lesen Sie?' Mick asked. Normally, he'd say *du*. First impressions, in this case but, worried him but.

Guy handed him his book. Mick took one look –*Tantric* something-or-other – 'n' alarm bells started. His bar of choc – to make things worse – had a strawberry-yoghurt filling.

Did Mick know about Tantrism? was the next question.

FUCKSAKE!

It *was* what he thought, wasn't it?

'Vaguely,' he answered.

Guy seemed to realise he didn't. He took back the book, found a particular page, returned it to Mick. Offered some chocolate while he was at it. Mick passed on the choc.

Ticket collector turned up again as he grappled with what he was readin.

'*Sonst jemand zugestiegen?*' Actor shook his head.

Mick still wasn't getting anywhere. The abstractions were the prob.

He decided to try 'n' bluff it. *Aha*, he said as he handed back the book.

'How'd you get into it, in the first place?' (Another bluff.)

He put down Janice, turned to face the guy. Just as well: he was about to get the whole story.

Chapter 1

detailed the guy's career to date. Mick recognised the patterns, had heard it all before. Only difference, this time, was: this time, it was Austria. Otherwise, it was the same old story: living and working in the capital. Working every waking hour. The joys and stresses of marketing, PR, thon kind of thing. Steep learning-curves. Rapid promotions. Money money money. Boy'd ended up well up the top Austrian agency, famous for his graphics. Folk had started coming to him directly, that's why he was freelance now. Agency job ended up being too much, he said – too much and yet too little, that is. '*Zu viel und gleichzeitig: zu wenig,*' he kept repeating, his accent making the irony sound even more ironic. Big bucks, little substance, little that was *real*, he insisted. That was when he answered a small ad. In the *Wiener* –

Chapter 2

followed, right on course. Guy insisted he was opting out: was looking for a *balance*, at least. For *detachment* from problems. *Relief* from anxiety. That was another thing about Austrians 'n' Germans: way they *intellectualise* everything! Mick soon found himself half-listening, only. He wasn't *convinced*. There the guy was, sure, in all his smart gear – didn't take much to imagine his lifestyle – 'n' yet his patter was all spirituality. Mysticism.

AYE RIGHT!

So while your man's givin it: hints of Hindu, Buddha; is talkin meditation, transcendental or otherwise; is even layin claim to a life-away-from-work of ascetic-fuckin-ism; Mick's busy imaginin him in a roomful of strangers; the birds scud-naked; the guys in sticky boxers; 'n' so pissed off is he wi the guy intellectualisin, he's havin a go, nearly. It's no as if they'll see each other again, sure.

He didn't but. He chickened out. Tried *telepathy* instead. It worked, mind you. Guy was cuttin to the chase now. He *travelled a lot*, he was sayin. 'Used to fly all the time to Bangkok – '

Mick's ears pricked up –

'Sometimes twice a year. Didn't stop to pack, even. Ye can buy what you need when you get there.'

Chapter 3

A catalogue had been delivered to Mick's flat once. Someone wi the same name in the same part of town must've asked for it by phone. He'd had to laugh when he thought of the Thai receptionist tryin to cope wi *McGlinchey*. No that she'd done much better wi the streetname. First half, alone, was nae use to the postman, no when there was the Gardens, a Place, an Avenue, a Terrace, a Road, 'n' a Crescent to choose from – flats, both sides, on each. Mick could just imagine the other McGlinchey's face. The poor bastard, denied his photies –

What Mick was thinkin must've been written all over him.

'We're not talking sex tourism,' Austrian was suddenly insistin.

'Perish the thought!' Mick tried to protest – too late but. He'd been too slow: phrase had come to him in English 'n' he'd struggled to find the German.

'*Wobei die Frauen*,' the guy began to concede –

The women? Mick's ears pricked up. This was what he was waiting for –

Your man'd just realised he didn't know Mick's name but.

'*Ich bin der Bernd, übrigens,*' he said, reaching across to shake hands. '*Und du?*'

'*Ich bin der Mick,*' – exaggerating the grip.

'*Mick,*' Bernd repeated. '*Die Frauen, sage ich dir, Mick –* '

He paused before delivering the verdict.

Mick's dick stirred.

'*Sex pur!*' he proclaimed.

It stirred again.

'*Ja, ja! Genau! Sex pur!*' Bernd repeated, nodding.

Mick would've been in there – if someone'd been offerin – like a shot.

Bernd had been less of a tart. Boy'd got involved, seriously involved, with one woman in particular. *Love*, it had been.

Okay, maybe I was harsh on him earlier. I take it all back. Well, maybe not *everything* –

Chapter 3 (again)

The woman had been like no other Bernd had ever been with.

Bangkok, they'd met in; but they'd moved back to her village. Off the map, it was. They'd communicated in English 'n' bits of French – though her English was worse than his, Bernd said. Mick spared him the nudge-nudge wink-wink, *the language of love* etc. Kind of patter Bernd would've got, had Gavin 'n' Duncan been here.

Mick was different, was surprising himself, even. He was *warming* to Bernd now. Was *touched* by the story. Wanted the boy to succeed.

At one point, Bernd had *had* to go home. To keep things ticking, he explained. He'd *sworn* he'd return and she'd trusted him. He'd *begged* her to visit him. '*Angefleht hab i sie,*' he said – he'd the balls 'n' all to admit it. He'd sent her a ticket soon as he landed, and better still: she'd come. Ye could see what it meant to him. Poor thing hadn't liked Austria, though. Wasn't just the climate, he stressed. And it was nothing to do with the size of Vienna – she'd handled Bangkok, sure. No, it was the *unfriendliness* of the people. 'The *racism*,' Bernd said. Ye could *see* it pained him. He spelt it out but: having her there had allowed him to see how racist the Austrians could be still.

The boy paused. His first serious pause –

The silence was embarrassing Mick. The love story had turned political, 'n' he didn't know what to do wi this: the honesty – *hurt* – in the air now.

It was strange how it was getting to him. It wasn't that Bernd's claim was new to him. Mick had written about this. He *knew* that after the war the Austrians had claimed they were innocent. Had blamed the Germans, making out they were victims. That, Mick *knew*. *Discussing* the matter was different but. Even if your man here was critical himself –

'*Rassismus ist doch ein großes Problem überall in Europa,*'

Mick tried to claim. '*Rassismus haben wir in England auch! In Schottland auch!*'

Bernd wasn't having it: 'Look at Haider,' he insisted. 'They're *voting* for bloody Haider. The Austrians are voting for Haider!'

Bernd sat for what seemed like forever; pain, more than anger, all over him. It wasn't a moment too soon for Mick when, finally, he returned to his story.

His lover had gone home early. Disappointed or not, he could *understand*, he said. That was the thing about this boy, Mick now realised: he was so bloody reasonable!

Five months later, as planned, he'd flown back again. The reception he got from her family & friends – from the *village*, he stressed – was better than ever. The *sex*, Bernd continued in his matter-of-fact way, was also the best ever. It was *more than that*, however. What they had – he and she – was *special*. What they didn't have was a long-term future. *Realistically speaking*, he couldn't see them together ten, twenty, years down the line.

Mick would've given his right arm to be able to argue; for some way of consolin the boy. He couldn't think of nuthin.

'*Had ve but vorld enough, and time*,' Bernd quoted, wistfully.

He realised too late, Mick, the words were meant to be English.

'*Wie bitte?*'

'*Had ve but vorld enough, and time*,' Bernd repeated.

He meant *world enough*. Mick was still clueless but.

Bernd was amazed. 'You are not knowing 'To His Coy Mishtress' from Andrew Marwell?' he asked – in English, suddenly.

Mick didn't: something else from where he came from he didn't know.

'Out of ze seventeenth century, but it functions ewery time,' Bernd informed him. 'Ven I read ze German translation to a voman, it functions ewery time. I am reading only one or two werses and ve are making love. No voman waits for ze zird werse.'

Mick laughed. 'Have to get a hold o that, then!'

The joke was lost on Bernd – who now switched back to German.

Mick – sensing the ending was coming – began to brace himself. Was as if, for the same reason, the whole carriage had hushed. Others, audible before, were suddenly silent.

The inevitable had happened, Bernd now told him: the night had come when, with a monsoon coming down outside, and them wrapped up in each other, her in his lap on the floor, she'd stopped nibbling the finger-food surrounding them and announced:

Tonight last night.

Tomorrow: Bernd GO!

It hadn't come as a surprise. He hadn't tried to argue. He'd respected what she said, he said, and they'd slipped easily, naturally, into love-sweet-love.

Some fuckin session, it must've been.

'So was *erleb i nie wieder,*' Bernd concluded.

'*Zy beauty vill no more be seen,*' he sighed.

There was another pause.

THE END?

Bernd staring ahead still; recalling. Mick managin not to say *Never say never, though, eh*; not to tell the one about the celibate Marketing Executive. Mick rememberin his own last time: Fiona perched above him, lettin the head in, not the rest; then gettin off 'n' askin could she watch him DIY; 'n' him thinkin *Way hey! Changed days, eh?* 'n' takin a deep breath 'n' goin for it; bit of bravado, like; bit of the male-stripper, bit of cheeky-chappy; showin her the odd stroke he'd wished she'd known in the first place; then comin, grand-style, no turnin away but, 'n' her sayin *Thanks*, soundin surprised even; as if she hadn't thought he'd it in him; no like that anyway; 'n' then the killer: way she'd thrown him out; told him to forget any ideas he had of sex-on-tap – *not with her, he hadn't*; told him that from tonight onwards, she'd take *great* pleasure in imaginin him DIYing an *thanks very much for the demo!*

Gob-smacked, he'd been. Total fuckin shoutin-match had followed. Hadn't made him any the wiser –

He looked up again, Mick, to see Bernd lookin concerned; on the verge of askin something. Mick asked his own question, quick.

'You two still in touch?'

Bernd looked as if he might still ask his question.

'Do you write at least?' Mick continued, in a panic. 'How long ago was all this?'

He'd guessed right. Seven or eight years had passed. Guy was still cut up but.

Letters had gone backwards 'n' forwards. For a matter of months but, only.

'Maybe it was too painful for her,' Mick suggested. His gentleness surprised him. Summit was tellin him but to tread carefully.

Bernd shook his head. That wasn't the reason. He paused and looked at Mick before revealing he'd received another letter. *Recently.*

AN EPILOGUE!

Mick was out of his seat nearly. On the verge of shaking the boy's hand, he was.

Then: it could be *bad* news, it struck him.

He waited.

Boy's next sentence started wi *beigelegt*; took ages to get to *Foto*.

'Of her?' Mick asked. Suspense was killin him.

'Is she as beautiful as ever?' he risked askin.

Bernd didn't answer. Not initially.

Eventually, he shook his head.

'*Ich habe einen Sohn,*' he said.

HOLY FUCKIN JESUS: HIM 'N' ALL?

'A seven-year-old?'

Bernd nodded.

Mick had guessed right. The letter was invitin him to the weeboy's birthday.

'And you'd no idea of the kid before?'

Bernd shook his head.

'Why didn't she tell you?'

Why the hell he nearly said.

'She'll have had her reasons.'

'Are you not furious?'

Furious could've turned the guy against him, he realised too late. He'd have to be more careful.

'I've no right to be.'

He was so bloody rational, reasonable, Bernd.

'But part of you must be?'

'No. She decided not to tell me. I respect that. She must have had her reasons.'

That phrase again: *Sie wird einen Grund gehabt haben.*

'So why tell you now, then?'

'Maybe now it is possible, and before it was not.'

'So she re-writes the script? Now that it suits her?'

For the first time, a look from Bernd showed he knew: Mick *disapproved*.

Mick changed tack. Had to.

'Surely it would only've been fair to inform you? To consult you?'

Bernd shook his head.

'Things change. We change. How we feel about things changes.'

'Are you going back for the party?'

Bernd nodded. 'Of course.'

'And what do you expect?'

Mick was beginning to wonder how personal he could get here.

'I expect nothing,' Bernd said – almost *stated*. 'I'll meet the boy. His mother wants me to. She writes that *he* wants to. Maybe we'll hit it off. Maybe we won't. We'll see.'

The guy was totally *composed* still.

'Would it not hurt not to? Hit it off, I mean – '

He *had* to ask.

'I haven't had a son to date. Nothing would've changed in that respect,' Bernd said.

He was so bloody *rational*.

'There is no existing relationship to miss.'

'But you would now *know*,' Mick protested. 'Would now have *met* him.'

'I'll settle for whatever happens.'

'And his mother?'

'I love her.'

'I can accept whatever happens.'

Wow.

Their journey wasn't over yet. In a way, the conversation was but. Mick tried to re-visit parts, to probe, poke, open up, dissect more. He ran various what-if-s by the boy; tried to. Bernd remained philosophical. He would always respect what the woman wanted. What she decided. She had had the child, not him, he insisted again. She'd brought him up alone. *Sie wird einen Grund gehabt haben.*

'Did you ever suspect she was pregnant?' Mick asked.

Bernd shook his head. 'She took care of that side of things,' he said.

For someone from a 'chiefly Catholic' country, he could be very matter-of-fact. Was so self-assured; so *open*.

'Except she didn't that last night,' Mick said. 'Or didn't towards the end.'

There was no reaction from Bernd.

'Are you not angry about that deception?'

He'd decided to risk the question. Soon as he used the D-word but, he feared an angry response.

The guy hardly blinked.

'I don't have a problem with that,' Bernd insisted. 'For me, it's not deception. If she wanted a baby, with me but without me, that's fine. She'll have had her reasons.'

It was pitch black outside now. A chance to see the Semmering Valley and Fischbacher Alps gone. That's what happened when trips became routine. You stopped looking, seeing. Started preferring a good book, or trying to get your reports done. Even to grab some kip.

Sie wird einen Grund gehabt haben – that these were Bernd's last words seemed right.

The silence in the compartment now minded Mick of Mass. The silence after the sermon.

The silence – miraculously – continued. It had been some conversation. Mick couldn't believe the ground they'd covered. The countries involved, no: the *continents*.

Bernd was breaking another strip of chocolate off. He broke it in two, placed one piece on his tongue, then – spotting Mick watching – offered him some. Mick, this time, accepted.

The chocolate got them off the big questions and onto Mick's trip. It was no time before the tannoy interrupted them but:

Meine Damen und Herren, wir erreichen in Kürze Graz Hauptbahnhof. Ladies and gentle men, ze next shtop: Graz Hauptbahnhof.

Sure enough: outside, if ye looked, there was a steadier flow of shops, houses, billboards.

As the train pulled in, the two of them stood up, started to pack their things. Mick watched in the window: how they made space for each other; were already parting, separating. When, in time, they shook hands, something told him Bernd felt *indebted*. It was hard to take – excruciating, almost – this credit for summit he'd not been, not done.

'*Alles, alles Gute, Mick,*' Bernd stressed, still not releasing his hand.

'*Ja, dir auch: alles Gute!*' Mick answered, giving an extra squeeze.

There was no attempt to exchange details. This was definitely it.

The End

'You go ahead, Bernd!' Mick urged. 'Don't worry about me.'

He tried to wave Bernd on. 'I'll take my time wi this,' he said, pointing to his case.

He felt a right bastard. Didn't want Bernd meetin the Hackls but.

Bernd was a light traveller.

'Oh – 'n' I hope the party goes well!' Mick called after him.

Bernd stopped, turned to face him again, nodded. Gave one last wave, then vanished.

It was a burdened Mick that toiled in his wake. Cursin himself grand-style again, he was. It wasn't for not acceptin Bernd's offer of help but. Nor was it to do wi Bernd no meetin the Hackls. No, as he struggled wi his case, he was strugglin wi summit else, Mick. Was strugglin wi why the fuck he'd not told Bernd about his own 'love-child' – pre-Fiona: the near-thing or false alarm, some years back – a point on which he had to trust its mother who, back then, had flown home alone.

And who, if Mick thought about it, wasn't a million miles away from where he was now.

16

Typical! *Bloomin* typical!

Even though they were back in Derry, Liam'd been quite happy, quite comfy, thank you very much. In a world of his own, he'd been, sitting reading on the landing, between the two portholes. And what happens? His Aunt Bernadette comes up the stairs, that's what happens: catches him, sees what the weeboy's doing, looks at him as if he'd a buckin screw loose.

'What are ye doin' in here, youngfella? Why aren't ye out in the sun? It's a sin before God, so it is: being inside on a day like this!'

Liam held his book up. 'I'm reading,' he said.

He could've tried asking her to let him. Something about the look on her face, the tone of her voice, and thon way she was standing over him told him he'd be wasting his time but. So he's just waiting for her to turf him out, when – God's my judge! – a miracle happens: all Bernadette did was *shrug* and say, 'Well away into the livingroom and at least sit on one of the good chairs. Your Granny O'Donnell didn't spend all that money on new furniture for you to sit on the stairs!'

It was a *total* miracle. Wee soul was so gobsmacked, was as if he was glued to the spot.

God knows how long Liam stayed there, the book open in front of him, before the snores out of his da, upstairs, brought him back to his senses. His da would've been snoring all along. Liam hadn't heard him but. The likes of Showaddywaddy must've drowned him out.

Once the weeboy did notice, it was no time before the snoring was browning him off. He'd to wonder sometimes why they bothered their arses going to Ireland, if all the lazy shite was goney do was sleep. It was beyond a friggin joke getting. Okay, so his da often had a long lie at weekends at home. Here but, it was every bloomin day, and everyone had to wait for him before they could go for a run. It wasn't fair. Not that there was any telling his da what was fair and what wasn't. He was the one bringing the money in. And that was that.

The problem was that their mother and father went over the border at night. They didn't go out until all hours, and Christ knows when they got back! Their mother, right enough, give her her due, would get up in the morning nevertheless and get the weans their breakfasts. She always done the dishes right away. She didn't want to have Gran or Bernie claiming they'd extra work. She even done *theirs*: 'It'll give your Aunt Bernadette a rest, sure!'

The weans, for their part, had their mother tortured. Every day, by eleven at the latest, they'd be asking where they were going? Bridget would come up wi a few possibilities. Buncrana, to the Amusements. Or Muff, for candy floss. By twelve, they'd be asking *when* they were goney go? 'Not long now, love. It won't be long now.' By one, they'd be wanting to know when their daddy was goney get up? By half one, was he not up yet? By two, *why* he wasn't up yet? And they'd start complaining that it *wasn't fair so it wasn't* – and by that point, Bridget, at the end of her tether, wouldn't give a damn no more and would say, 'Away and make him a mug of tea and see if that gets him up!' And they would compete to make the tea, and fight over who was to carry it, and one of them would always come back down wi the bacon & eggs Bridget had made at ten – untouched. Sooner or later (the big lump had to get up sometime), they'd come running down and report, 'Daddy says he's gettin up now, Mum. He says he's getting up now!'

'We're goin to Buncrana! Daddy says we're goin to Buncrana!'

'And I'm to get sittin in the front!'

'Naw, you're not. Daddy said it was my turn yesterday. Mum, TELL him!'

And Liam, who always sat behind his mother so as not to be squashed, would know they weren't away yet, cos their da would come down in his vest and trousers, and he'd have to have a wash and a shave still, and then he'd want another cup of tea and a smoke. And if they were really unlucky, he'd need to go for a sit. *A sit with a silent haitch*, as their Uncle Dermot called it. Liam would hide the *Journal*, to try and speed things up.

The worst thing that could happen was not getting away before their gran's home-help arrived. If they didn't get away by then, they'd be stuck in the house for another hour. Their da had the gift of the gab, ye see, he never shut up, and Philomena Devlin encouraged him just. She thought he was great craic – always had been, even when they were growing up – and she'd leave again at half four whether her work was done or not.

'You're not paid to listen to our Liam, ye know,' Gran would give off.

'Aye, right, Missus O'Donnell. Aye, right, I heard ye, sure.'

Still, if it hadn't've been for Philomena, they'd never've heard about the hypnotist.

She comes in this afternoon, the O'Donnells had been over about ten days at the time, and she says, 'Yes, Bridget! Yes, Liam! Hello there, Missus O'Donnell – how are you today? Yes, weans!'

Liam's mother and father said, 'Yes, Philomena!' back, and 'How's the form?' They never talked like that, back in Scotland.

'So what was the craic like last night?' Philomena asks. 'Was it good?'

'Aye, it wasn't bad,' says Bridget.

Liam had heard his mum talking about the hypnotist that morning. She'd not given away much: just that she'd sat on her hands, terrified. 'Aye, well I don't agree wi it at all,' Gran had said. 'It's the work of the Devil, that's what it is!' His mum had got her arse out of the road before there was any awkward questions.

His da, unlike his mum, was raving about it; just raving about it. 'Aw, it was *brilliant*, Philomena,' he says. 'We really enjoyed ourselves!'

'Who did yis go wi, again?'

'Well, it was me and Bridget. And our Fergus and his Eileen. And do you know ma nephew, our Roisin's second eldest, Damien?'

'Aye.'

'Well it was him and his wife as well. We just took the one car.'

'And was it that place in Muff? Is that the one?'

'Aye, just over the border. Farrell's, it's called.'

'Farrell's! Aye, that's the name I was trying to mind! Wha'd'ye think – I might be going there tonight!'

'Naw! And is it the hypnotist ye're going to see?'

'Aye.'

'Aw well, you'll enjoy it so you will. Won't she, Bridget?'

'Aye.'

'Although Bridget here was terrified, weren't you, love?'

'Aye, I'd ma rosary beads in ma right hand the whole time, Philomena, clinging to the crucifix.'

'Aw, I'm like you, Bridget, love. I'll be petrified.'

'Sure there's nothing to it!' their da said. 'You don't need to go up on stage, sure.'

'Just you sit on your hands, Philomena, when he tells you to join them!' Bridget said. 'That's what I done. That way he can't get at you!'

'Who are you going wi, anyway?'

'A few o my sons. Five of us are going over in the car.'

Liam knew that Philomena's husband had been killed in the Troubles. That's why she was Gran's home-help: she needed the money. Her sons – seven, she had – were said to be bad brutes; right Republicans.

'Well, you'll enjoy it,' his da assured her. 'It's good craic!'

'So what does he do, lik?' Philomena asked.

'Och, we'd only spoil it for you,' Bridget answered.

'Naw, go on, tell us a wee bit!' Philomena said. 'Jist to whet my appetite!'

The weans spotted their mum looking at their da. She was trying to warn him their gran didn't approve. Just biding her time before she pounced, the woman was.

Their da knew fine what the look meant; carried on regardless but. 'Well he comes on,' he said, 'and he's lik: "I am the great Robin Wills" and all that stuff. And then he goes on about the history of hypnotism, trying to make it sound all mysterious. He's a bit of a know-all at times, to be honest.'

You could see the disappointment on Philomena's face.

'He's good once he gets going, though,' Bridget said, to reassure her.

'And then he gets the whole audience to join its hands, just the fingertips, lik – '

'Aye, I wouldn't but – '

'And concentrate and press really hard. And he says things. And then when he's finished, anyone whose fingers are stuck together has to go up on stage.'

'Aye, and Damien, Roisin's boy, had to go up!'

'Did he now?' (That was Gran.) 'First I've heard of that. Ye didn't tell me that this morning, Bridget McCluskey! I'm always saying thon youngfella's no' religious enough –'

'So what happened to him, Mum?'

Ciara had blurted it out before she could help herself. The weans all glared at her. They knew fine they shouldn't be listening; that now they might not get to hear the story.

Sure enough: 'Are yous *listening*?" Bridget asked. 'This isn't for your ears. Away outside and play with yourselves!'

'Och, leave them alone, Bridget. They're all right where they are!' their da insisted. 'It'll not do them any harm.'

'So what did happen to Damien?'

Philomena wanted to know an' all.

The weans relaxed, began to settle down again.

'Och, nothing. He was up on stage the whole time. When it came to the end but, the hypnotist just kept ten of them for the finale and sent the rest back down. So Damien just came back to us and sat down.'

'And had he been asleep?'

'I'm not sure. I think he only puts you in a deep sleep if he's going to use you.'

'Are you sure he didn't get to you, Da?' Liam asked.

'Aye, why?'

'Cos you never got out of your bed until two this afternoon, that's why!'

Everyone laughed. Their da gave Liam a filthy look. 'That's enough of that, you. Right? Cheeky pup.'

'So what kinda thing did he have them doing then?'

You could see Philomena was impatient, getting.

'I don't want to spoil it for you,' their da said, 'it was very good but. Lik: he took the first boy and put him to sleep. And then he sat him on a bar-stool and told him he was on a horse, he was riding a horse. And first he had him doing a gentle saunter, and then a bit of a trot, and then a gallop and finally, a mad gallop,' their da was laughing at the thought, 'and you should've seen the boy acting it all out on the stool!!' He did a quick impersonation and everyone laughed. 'Aye, it was very good so it was.'

Everyone was laughing. Even their gran.

Sean, as usual, imitated his da: 'And then a mad gallop!' and had what looked like an epileptic fit before he fell to the floor.

'And what else did he make them do?'

'I don't want to ruin it on Philomena, but he gave them onions to eat and told them it was apples –'

'And did they eat them?' Ciara asked.

'Aye, they were really getting stuck into them, and honest to God –'

'Leave God out of it, you! God's got nothing to do with it,' Gran said. 'It's against your religion, in fact. It's up that road to confession ye should be going, not sitting here keeping that one back from her work!'

'Och, Ma, give over! There's no harm in it, sure. Honestly, Philomena, I'm no' jokin ye: they were munching these bloody big onions and Wills was asking them what they tasted lik? And they were all saying: lovely. Gorgeous. Never tasted apples lik them in their lives. And the audience were killing themselves, weren't they, Bridget?'

Bridget was laughing too much to be able to answer.

'The best one was the finale but,' their da started.

'Wha'd he do?' Philomena asked.

'Naw, don't be telling Philomena that bit, Liam,' Bridget said. 'You'll only spoil it on her, sure.'

'Och, just go ahead, Liam. It's no odds. I hear he changes it every night anyway. There's ones goes back and back.'

'Naw, *don't*, I said, Liam!' Bridget said. 'I'm telling you not to!'

She tried to nod at the weans and his mother who was watching him like a hawk. Their da wasn't having it but. Too good a story, it was. 'Sure there's no harm in it, woman!'

He waved Philomena over. 'C'm'ere tay I tell you how it started. To do wi bellybuttons, it was.'

The weans laughed. They couldn't wait. Bellybuttons!

Their da could hardly whisper into Philomena's ear for laughing. Philomena was laughing, too; thon dirty kind of laugh.

Liam could hear some of it: Adam and Eve – Adam created in God's own image – navel-less – sexual reproduction.

'Right, that's enough of that talk in my house, you!' Gran objected.

'Naw, Mother. It's not dirty – honest!' their da said. And he quoted the hypnotist out loud. This bit was obviously okay. '"The navel is a mark of our fallen state. So tonight, ladies and gentlemen, I shall take you back to the time before Adam and Eve's expulsion from Eden!" – and he turns to the ten on stage and tells them they'd lost their bellybuttons!'

'And they believed him!' Bridget roared, now able to find it funny again.

'Aye, and they were tearing open their shirts and their blouses and staring at their stomachs. And the whole audience could see their stomachs and their bellybuttons. They were all convinced they'd lost them but!'

'Aye, and one woman, God love her, was crying her eyes out cos she thought she'd lost hers!'

The weans were wetting themselves, laughing. Sean pulled up his T-shirt in mock dismay. 'Aw Good God Almighty!' he squealed. 'My bellybutton's disappeared!' Ciara didn't know whether she was laughing at him or at her da. She was sore laughing but.

'I WANT MY BELLYBUTTON BACK! RIGHT NOW!' their da boomed, impersonating someone. 'And some o them were getting right and angry,' he explained. 'Aggressive, lik. And they were going up to each other and saying, "Have you got my bellybutton?" – "Aye, ye have so!" – "Give it back to me, you, or I'm going to hit you a thump!" And they were tearing the clothes off each other, they were. And one woman had no bra on, and Wills had to jump to cover her up!'

'That's filthy, you!' Gran complained. She was laughing herself but.

'No bra on!' Sean repeated.

His mother hit him a slap. 'That's enough, you!'

'Leave him alone, Bridget. There's no need for that!' his da protested.

Ciara and Annette looked at each other, and Annette shook her head in disgust. It was just like their da to defend the boys, specially if it was to do wi something dirty. Ciara was about to open her mouth to say something when Philomena started choking – her smoker's cough.

Their da wasn't finished yet: 'And then he sends them down into the audience and tells them to find their bellybuttons!' he continued. '*Someone* must have them, he said. And you want to have seen the ten o them descending on the audience. And they were jumping on people, so they were! And tearing their shirts open! And then turning away, all disappointed. "Naw, thon's not my bellybutton!" And this big lump of a woman comes up to Damien Doherty and says, "*You* stole ma bellybutton, didn't you, ye bugger ye? Tell the truth, now!" And he's lik: "Naw, I didn't, Missus, I swear to God I didn't" but she wasn't for believing him and she tore open his shirt, and I'm no' kidding ye: God Almighty, you want to see the hair on thon youngfella's stomach, he's pure black, disgustin, he is! Well, doesn't she take one look at him and say, "Naw, that can't be ma bellybutton, now, it's far too buckin hairy!"'

Liam saw his mother blushing. Then she spoke up, as if to change the subject. 'Ye know, I'm sure that Wills boy let some of them go home, without finding them.'

'That's terrible!' Gran said.

The weans were all gutting themselves, by this stage. Someone set them all off again any time they stopped. The wee ones were laughing an' all, but looking at their mother or father but, as if they weren't sure what the joke was. The big ones were apo-bloody-plectic, nearly; turning different shades of beetroot. You could see Liam's sides were killing him. Annette was pure choking. Ciara was clutching her sides – it obviously wasn't helping but. 'Can you imagine it?' she finally managed to shriek.

Their da took one look at them all laughing, then grinned to himself and winked at Philomena. She was obviously thinking what a comedian, what amazing craic, Big Liam O'Donnell still was: Scotland had done nothing to change him.

The next day the weans couldn't wait for Philomena to arrive, to hear what the hypnotist had got up to when she went. Their poor mother heard nothing all morning but, 'When's Philomena coming, Mum?' – 'Is Philomena coming soon, Mum?'

For once, their da got out of bed before one o' clock. They'd be away in the car by two at this rate. The weans started stalling. Liam let his da have the *Journal* when he went for a sit. Ciara deliberately fell and cut herself so she'd need a stickin plaster. They had to find them first. Their gran couldn't understand why the plasters weren't where she'd left them (Annette had hidden them). And when it looked as if they'd soon be setting out, Sean sneaked out and let the tyres down. The neds up the street would get the blame.

Finally, Philomena showed. She hadn't been able to get a bus. They'd burned one out on Shipquay Street again.

The weans went running up to her.

'Yes, Philomena!' – 'Yes, Sean, son!'

'Yes, Philomena!' – 'Yes, Ciara, love!'

Liam noticed they were all talking like that now. Even the wee ones. Not even two weeks over, and they were all 'all Derry' already.

Sean tripped over Annette on the way in. She hit him a slap. 'See you, weeboy? I'm goney hit ye a thump so I am if ye don't watch!'

'C'mon, weans, currit out. There's no call for that, now,' Philomena said.

They followed her into the livingroom where their mother and father were saying cheerio before they left.

'So what was the craic like last night, Philomena?' Ciara blurted out.

Philomena looked at her, then at her father and mother. Bridget laughed. 'The hypnotist! They've been waiting all day to hear about it!'

'Aw naw!' Gran groaned. 'That one's never going to get any work done if yis start thon carry-on again!'

'Did he do the sact same again?' Annette asked.

'Aw, love, do me a favour and don't ask! Sure all I remember is the finale – '

She spotted the cheeky look their da was giving her. 'And naw, I wasn't drinking, Liam, before ye make any comment – '

'Was it the bellybuttons again, Aunt Philomena?'

'*Aunt* Philomena???' Sean mouthed to Liam. Ciara was obviously hoping sooking up might get the story out of her.

Philomena knew she'd have to concede defeat. It was written all over her: she'd have to give in and tell them.

'Naw, love, he didn't do the bellybuttons last night, love. It was a different finale last night. And wha' d'ye think: our Seamus was up on stage!'

'Oh God, was he?'

'Aye.'

The weans all sat down, quick. Wherever a space could be found.

'So what happened? Wha'd the hypnotist do to him?' Ciara asked.

'Well, when it came to the end, didn't Wills take the ten left on stage, and he took their hands and pretended to place their own individual leprechauns into each of their palms.'

Philomena could see the weans were loving it. She herself couldn't find it one bit bloody funny but.

'Aye,' she continued, 'and he told them that this was Paddy, their very own leprechaun, their own personal leprechaun, and he warned them to take very special care of him. And right enough, God love them, you want to have seen them all: they were all patting him and saying things like: "Hello, Paddy. How are ye doing? I'm Patricia, and I'm going to look after you from now on, so I am!"'

The weans were chuckling already. Cahal was pestering his mother. 'Mum, can I have ma own wee leper on?' Ciara had a giggling fit when she heard him.

'And one boy was wasting no time at all: he was already asking Paddy where his pot of gold was buried and could they go there together some time? The audience was in stitches, right enough.'

Everybody laughed.

'And what about your Seamus?' Ciara asked. 'Wha'd he do?'

'Oh, his wee Paddy spent no time at all in his hand before he jumped off and run away!'

'So wha'd Seamus do? Run after him, like?' Gran asked. She sounded right sarcastic.

Cahal piped up again. 'Mum, the leper on runned away, Mum!'

'Aye, son!' Bridget said, brushing his wee hand away and telling him to shoosh, that she needed to concentrate. Something told her something terrible was coming.

'Not right away, Missus O'Donnell,' Philomena said, to answer their gran. 'He turned to the hypnotist, all upset like, Seamus, and he said, "Can I have another one, Mister? Mine run away!" And Wills looked at him and said, "Well you'd better bloody well go running after him, squire, cos it's *your* leprechaun, and if anything happens to Paddy, you're in Big Trouble!" So our Seamus runs after it, right enough, and a couple of minutes later, he's back on stage again, tugging the hypnotist's sleeve lik he used to tug my skirt, God love him. And he's telling the hypnotist everything's okay, that he found wee Paddy again – '

Their da was killing himself. 'I wish I'd seen it! Your Seamus! A grown man! And Paddy the Leprechaun!'

Bridget was reluctant to laugh. There was *definitely* something about Philomena that told her something was wrong.

'So did anything else happen?' Ciara, again.

'Not bloody half, love!' Philomena looked at Gran. 'If you'll excuse ma language, Missus O'Donnell. Weren't they allowed to take their leprechauns home, if you don't mind!'

'So did Paddy make it past Customs?' their da asked. Lapping the story up, he was, blind to what Bridget saw. Bridget wanted to signal to him to shut the buck up, wee Cahal was still pestering her but: 'Mum, you see! You can so take a leper on home!'

Their da suddenly stopped laughing. The smile went to the other side of his face. 'There's something wrong, Philomena, isn't there, love? Did something happen?'

'Aye, on the way home. You should've seen it!' she said, running her hand round the back of her head. 'God, it was terrible,' she said. 'The five of us got into the car. Our Calum was driving, and Seamus got into the passenger seat wi Paddy the Leprechaun. And God love the youngfella, he really was looking after him, talking away to him, he was, promising him the world – '

'So what went wrong?' Ciara asked, all worried. 'Don't tell me some smart-arse did something to Paddy?'

Ciara had a soft spot for Seamus. He'd lovely eyes, she thought, *plus* he was the best dresser among the Devlin brothers, *by far*. 'Like Donny Osmond – wi a Derry accent but' was what she told her pals, back home.

'No, love. It wasn't nothing lik that there. Naw, we got to the border, sweetheart, and the soldiers pulled the car over. We always get searched cos of what my Bernard, God rest his soul, is supposed to have done before the paratroopers murdered him. Anyway, our Calum had to put the window down to show them his driving licence. And that's when Paddy jumped out – '

Liam was biting his cheeks, trying not to laugh. Ciara, meanwhile, was patting Philomena, to comfort her.

'And that was bad enough, but here, our Seamus opens the car door and races out after him. Calum tried to stop him, couldn't but. And all I hears, in a posh English accent, is, "STOP, or we'll shoot! Stop or we'll bloody SHOOT" And Jaysus, Mary and Joseph, I was having a heart attack, nearly. Swear tay God I was.'

The weans had all stopped laughing, except Annette who looked as if she was about to bloody well explode. Ciara, whose eyes had filled up, hit her a slap. 'It's not one bit funny, you!'

'They didn't shoot but,' they were relieved to hear. 'They must've realised he wasn't armed. Our Seamus but's running round the checkpoint, shouting, "Paddy, would you come here! I'm warning ye now! That's the last time I'm going to tell ye: come here!" They set an Alsatian loose on him.'

Annette giggled, despite herself.

'And it bit a lump out of the youngfella's arse! Excuse ma language, Missus O'Donnell!'

Sean reached for his right buttock. 'Owyah! Ma bum!' he groaned.

'That's enough, you!' his da warned. 'Or your bum *will* be sore!'

Philomena waited for them to quieten. 'The worst of it is: the youngfella's up in court in November for misbehaving at a checkpoint. I can't remember what they call what they've got him on.'

'I hope to God he gets away with it, whatever it's called,' Bridget said. 'You'll have to write and tell us what happens.'

Despite her promises, Philomena didn't write. Or rather: no matter how often the weans asked, no letter arrived.

At first, their da would've said the case wasn't up yet, 'That won't be up yet. Sure it takes time for them things to work their way through.' When the weans continued to pester him, he said it wouldn't be this side of Christmas. In January, their mother claimed it 'might even be after Easter, sure'. The last Wee Liam minds it being mentioned, his mother and father said the case could've been dropped for all they knew. The weans weren't satisfied, begged them to phone Derry to find out. They never ever got an answer but.

All Liam remembers is at some point being minded of the wee dog they'd had in Derry, up to the time he started school. Rover was its name. When the day came that Rover took sick, their da took him to the vet. He came back that night without Rover, and said the dog was in hospital. When the weans asked when he was getting out, their da said Tuesday. On the Tuesday but, there was still no Rover. Their da said not to worry, they'd be getting him back on Friday. That's what their mammy said, too. There was no Rover the following Friday either but, nor the one after that, and the Friday after that, when their da came back from work, Ciara overheard their mammy saying it was no good, the weans weren't going to forget about him, and that was when her and Annette got taken into the scullery and told Rover was *dead*.

Liam minds his da having already moved onto something else by the time he came in for *Crackerjack*. He minds seeing his da wi one of his shoes on the anvil, hammering nails into the heel, and Annette and Ciara busy trying to tell him Rover was *dead*. He minds not knowing what *dead* meant, sensing but it wasn't good. He also minds thinking it wasn't right, wasn't fair, that his sisters – who were younger than him – found out before him what *dead* was. He minds, too, his mother and father then having to admit that people *die* also – Ciara it was, who asked – and he minds them rushing to explain it was okay but, that when you died, you went up to Heaven which was the most beautiful place you could imagine, and there, you got to be with God the Father and the Baby Jesus and all the angels and saints – and everybody in your family who'd died. The weans didn't know anyone who'd died but, just wanted to know would *Rover* get into Heaven? At that point, their mother'd looked at their father lik he was the expert and he'd said only human beings got into Heaven because animals didn't have souls. Then he said: 'Right, that's it. That's enough. No more questions! Away an' give me peace to fix my shoes!' And at that, he took the shoe that was on the anvil off – and put the other one on.

17   the ancients

[*Enter* THE ANCIENTS, *en route to the* POOLSIDE]

This morning again, the ancients take up position just as I'm eating my last bites of breakfast. I prefer to stay indoors – not to eat on the terrace – though the louts of last week have flown home now. The ancients, who replaced them, strain to talk round the stairwell as they begin to sit down on the sunbeds.

'We've not got a *toaster* either,' the auld guy complains. 'Have you got a toaster?'

From his reaction, her-next-door clearly doesn't.

'Ye'd think ye'd have a toaster, wouldn't ye?' his wife begins to reason. 'We can't get no toast or nuthin!' he buts in but.

Her-through-the-wall mustn't answer. Worse still: maybe can't see the problem.

'Aye, and have you got a *kettle*?' he continues.

Your woman has been able to make do.

'Aye, heat it in pans, aye!' he repeats, sounding angry. 'But have ye got a *kettle*? That's what I asked.'

'Naw!' he repeats, as if to say, '*See*?!'

He pauses, looks at her – just timing the announcement:

'They *have* them, though, ye know!'

He's got her this time.

'Oh aye. They have them, alright. Over there – '

He nods to Reception in the corner.

'Ye have to *pay* for them but – '

'Pay for them!' his wife echoes. 'Have ye ever heard the like? Imagine having to pay for the likes of a kettle and a toaster – '

'It's no' right,' says he. All he does but is scratch at his knee.

The silence continues.

Time was, he'd've read them the riot act. His wife, whoever saw her, would've joined him. No' now but. He's too frail got.

He takes off his T-shirt. Picks at his chest, sitting up on the sunbed.

His wife, on her feet still, unbuttons the blouse she wears over her T-shirts.

He turns to the neighbour again. 'Last place we were in, they gave ye everything!'

'*Every*thing!' his wife confirms.

'We'd a kettle. A toaster. Ye didn't have to pay for nuthin. There was even a grill, wasn't there?'

'Aye, a lovely grill. Ye know: to do the bacon under – '

'We can't do our bacon here!' the husband protests.

His glasses shake on his nose as he looks round and up to the neighbour.

His eyes are skelly. Even from a distance, they look skelly.

Your woman must've mentioned the pans again.

'Oh no! I'm no' allowed no pans!' the wife says. 'Everything I eat has to be grilled – '

Another silence. This time, it could even be final.

'Lovely day yesterday!' the wife says, eventually, putting the blouse back on that she's just taken off.

She doesn't look at your woman. Speaks over her shoulder. Embarrassed, as she re-does her buttons.

'Yesterday was nice!' she tries, again, when she doesn't get a response.

Your woman must've agreed.

The auld guy takes over again: 'Where are ye from, love?'

It's like he's trying to placate her.

'Edinburgh!' he repeats when she tells him.

Means something to him, looks like.

'Lot of Irish in Edinburgh!' his wife says. She's strangely proud of the fact. Again, doesn't get a response but.

'And when did ye come over?' he asks, to smooth the path.

'Thursday? Aye – same as us! And when do ye go back?'

'The 6th? Aye! Same as us!'

He picks at his chest again; his skin as ashen as the T-shirt beside him. Question is, what the sun'll do. No sign of him using protection.

'When we got here, there wasn't a bus or nuthin, ye know! Not a bus, not a rep, in sight. Nuthin!'

They're back on track. This time, he gets the response he wants.

'Aye! A disgrace! Isn't it? We had to get a taxi up here, ye know!'

'Aye, had to take a taxi!' his wife echoes.

'Arrecife to here's no' cheap either!'

It's more and more noticeable how their comments overlap. Her voice is strong, whereas he talks through slipping teeth, it sounds like.

Sometimes, the two voices marry.

He fixes the glasses on his nose again, turns to the neighbour.

'Course, I'm made of money, me!!' he says, laughing suddenly and winking at her. His glasses go haywire.

'Aye, we're *loaded*!' his wife jokes, too. 'I'd just like to know where it all is! Where it all goes to. That's what I'd like to know!'

Your woman must laugh at this, and all.

The old guy's obviously encouraged.

'Give ye a laugh,' he says. 'We went to that Christmas Dinner yesterday. We'd put our names down, ye know. Anyway, I goes up to the boy at the end, to pay, like, and he says, There's *nothing to pay*! You've already paid, Sir! And I looks at him lik that and says, I'm sorry, but I haven't paid nuthin. And he looks down and checks his papers and says, According to this, Sir, you have. And then he says, Mr Donaghue, Sir? And I says, Yes – And he looks at me as if to say, There ye go! the boy does. But *I* looks at *him* and *I* say, Aye, but *which* Mr Donaghue? Might there be another one? And he looks, and sure enough, there was!'

He laughs. His wife chuckles, too; her face lighting up for the second time. 'Would ye credit it? Wasn't there two Mr Donaghues!'

At that, they both lie down to sunbathe; him fidgeting more to get himself comfortable.

Your woman's maybe grabbed the chance to make herself scarce.

They're side-by-side now. Him in his trunks, less and less to fill them. Her in her blouse, top and shorts. She looks that *solid*; good for a few nights at the Bingo yet.

Lying down, he looks frailer still. His hair thin; like it's wilting.

He's probably just lying there, thinking, remembering; enjoying the sun, maybe even. He looks like he will when he's laid out but.

'Sean and Patricia went to Edinburgh, didn't they?' he says, after a bit. A brave bit.

He doesn't open his eyes to talk.

He *sounds* frailer, now he's lying down, and all.

'Aye, right enough, they did,' says she – just as ye might've thought she wasn't goney answer.

'*They* died young, too, didn't they?' says he.

'Mm,' she murmurs, in the sun.

'Fifties. In his fifties, he only was. Sean. She was, too.'

'Mm.'

'And here's us still going – '

'Mm.'

She sounds relaxed; peaceful. Like she's enjoying herself.

'Here! Maybe they're trying to kill us off here!' he laughs. 'Maybe that's what they're at! Maybe they're hoping we'll fade away to nuthin!'

She turns to face him, laughing. Gutting herself, she is, behind her big round glasses. When she's done, she lies back down again.

'It'll take more than that, but, ay??!!'

He can hardly speak, himself, for choking.

They lie there, obviously settling for the complex again. Ye wouldn't believe there's an island out there. A volcano. The Papagayo beaches.

Supermercado's about as far as the auld guy's got. And who knows if she's been that far.

'How many o' a family did Sean and Patsy have again?'

Like he's been lying there, trying to remember.

She struggles and all, so he starts to answer his own question.

'There was Sean, the eldest – '

'Aye.'

'And then Paddy – '

'Mm.'

'And then Roisin – '

'God, aye, Roisin!'

A cleaner passes with her bucket; a local. They're not even aware of her.

'And then – '

He's starting to struggle, himself; to slow down.

'Marie!' he remembers, just as he might've been bate.

'And – young Tony!'

He's pleased wi remembering that one. You can see it.

Another pause, then: 'And the last wee one, her mother's double, God love her: Siobhan!'

His wife doesn't say nothing. He smiles, clears his throat, wriggles on the sunbed; stretches, flexes, then, finally, lies at peace.

'*Edinburgh*, eh?'

Like it's his final word on the matter.

[*Switch to* KITCHEN]

I clear away my breakfast things. Strangely choked as I rinse the dishes.

I'll chew on this for long enough –

No denying it: I know, deep down, I'll chew on it. And for long enough.

thorny one 18

One summer when he went over, Liam's cousin Una was running to Mass every day, and most days, while she was at it, she'd go to Confession an' all. When his Gran mentioned this to Liam, his Uncle Dermot, who was also in the room at the time, looked at him, winked, and said, 'What I'd lik to know's how come the weegirl's got so much to confess!' Liam's Gran said naw but, it wasn't that at all. 'I think she's got a crush on thon lovely new wee priest myself! That's what I reckon.'

It seems all the weemin in the parish were very keen on Father McIlroy – Father *Pat*, as they were allowed to call him – sure he always gave a lovely sermon, and if truth be told, he was a wee sweetheart. 'God knows where the Bishop found him!' Liam's Gran was forever saying. He was one of them new, modern priests, a *Charasmatic*, was a great one for keeping the light on during Confession and asking if he could know your name – and if you wanted to, you could even go round to his side of the *parteeshun* and sit opposite him in a chair. Liam's cousin Una was all for this, it seems. Couldn't get enough of it, she couldn't.

'She'll be asking him to put the kettle on next!' Liam said, hoping that if he made a joke of it, his gran wouldn't see he was nervous. Into himself but, he thought: You'd never get that back in Scotland! And: Thank Christ for that. The gimmicks *Father Pat* was getting up to didn't sound one bit like the religion Liam was brought up in. Liam would shit himself if the priest turned the light on, he knew he would. He didn't tell his gran that but. She'd only've asked him why? What a youngfella like him had to be afraid of?

The day his Gran came out wi all this, his Aunt Maureen – Una's mother – looked in in the afternoon for a cuppa tay.

'Aw, I could kill a cuppa tay, Mother,' she said, coming in the door.

'Aye, well you know where the kettle is!' Gran answered.

Maureen looked for a minute at Liam, as if she might ask him. He looked back at her but in a way that stopped her, and she just went into the kitchen.

'I was telling Liam here about your Una having a saft spot for wee Father Pat and always running to Mass,' his gran shouted through to her.

Maureen came back in, drying her hands with the dishcloth. 'Naw, Mother, it's not that, not that at all. Honest to God, it's not. Things lik that would never enter our Una's head, sure. Naw, she's genuine, I swear to God she is. She always was a wild holy wee-girl, sure. You know that yourself, now. You don't need me to tell you that!'

It seems that shortly before Liam went over, Una had a wild problem at the school. She was doing her A-level English, and the teacher had given her a book to read. It wasn't that *Lady Chatterbox's Lover*, it was something lik that but. Liam's Gran couldn't mind the name of it, not for the life of her. 'Never mind. It'll come back to me sure,' she assured him. There was a priest in it, that much she could mind.

It appears Una couldn't read the book because some of the things in it were against her religion – and the weegirl was in a wild state, so she was, since she needed it for her exams, and the Master had given her homework to do, worksheets an' all. Anyway, she was so upset, eventually she went to Liam's Aunt Maureen and said, 'Mammy, I've to read this here book for school – and I can't! It's full of dirty bits!'

It seems the weegirl was breaking her heart, so Maureen decided to sit down and try and read it herself. She hardly got as far as the bottom of the second page of the bit Una opened the book at but, before she was so disgusted she got on a bus and went straight up to her mother's. Part of the problem was that even in the opening pages a petticoat and frilly knickers were coming off – and that was just the wean in the book's doll they were talking about! It sounded that dirty but. The really disgustin thing was: later on in the book, the priest knew about the weegirl having her period and talked to her about it. That was the bit that upset Una, the bit she opened the book at for her mother, and the bit Maureen was holding open when she arrived up-to-high-doh at her mother's front door.

Liam's Gran had never heard tell of the book or the writer. 'It can't be that bad but, if they're giving her it to read at school,' she said. 'Leave it here wi me and I'll have a look at it, sure.'

The first page, alone, of the bit that got to Una most was more than enough for Liam's Gran, it turned out. 'Jaysus, Mary and Saint Joseph!' she shouted out of her when she read it, she told Liam. 'Thon's disgusting!' She'd been on the verge of heading straight up the street and confronting the Principal herself: 'I swear tay God I was. Ready to give him hell I was!' Something had stopped her but. She'd decided to play safe, to give it to her youngest son's wife first, to see what she thought of it; maybe Geraldine would see something in it they didn't, what with her being that bit younger an' all. His Gran wanted to be sure, lik, before marching up to the school.

Even the paragraph at the top of the offending double-page

was too much for Eugene's Geraldine. She brought the book straight back up to Liam's Gran. 'My God, Mrs O'Donnell!' she said. The poor weegirl was mortified. 'That there's the work of the Devil! *I* could never read that! Poor Una! What are they thinking of, giving the wean that? It's a sin before God, so it is'.

By this stage in the proceedings, his Gran had obviously been enjoying the craic (Liam could see it in her eyes, even if she was making out she'd been *black affronted*). She'd been unable to resist giving the book a final chance – and had given it to Rosemary, Sean, her second youngest's wife.

Rosemary's reaction soon had the whole family wondering what her and Sean got up to when they were on their own. She thought the book was *terr*ific: read it from cover to cover and announced it was great. 'I can see, right enough, what yous were offended about,' she said quickly when she saw the suspicious looks she was getting. 'Yous should stick wi it but. It all works out in the end. The priest *is* tempted – and aye, right enough, he does sleep wi her. He sticks wi his religion in the end but – '

Even when his Gran had told him all that, Liam couldn't say he'd heard tell of the book. Nor was he any the wiser when, that afternoon, Maureen supplied the name of it. If truth be told: the youngfella was just grateful they'd ended up going on about the book and had got off the subject of going to Confession.

•

It's funny how times change. A couple of years later it was a totally different story, a different story altogether. The bingo halls of Derry were empty, *deserted*, for Christ's sake, when the TV series they made of the book was shown. For however many weeks it was on, you couldn't've sold a bingo book on a Wednesday night in Derry, you know. Swear to God you couldn't've.

They all stayed in to watch it in Liam's Gran's house, too – so much so Liam knew not to try and phone on a Wednesday night, that it was a case of God-help-him, that he'd get a dog's abuse, if he made the mistake of phoning when their programme was on. His gran and his aunts were *loving* the series, were lapping it all up: the same ones, whoever saw them, as had got their knickers in a twist about the book. Liam knew, too, that Una – who hadn't ended up going away to be a nun after all – made a point of heading up to her granny's wi her mammy every Wednesday to watch it. Liam didn't watch it himself, each time he saw it on but, in the lounge of his bed-sit in Kelvinbridge, he could just imagine themmins sitting up in the Creggan watching it – and the craic afterwards, wi them all quarrelling over who'd been the first to think Richard Chamberlain made a beautiful priest.

19   a Protestant Catholic

There was only one thing worse than a Protestant – 'n' that was a lapsed *Catholic*. That's what he was reared up thinkin, Jim Kane.

●

Even as he mounted the steps, he still wasn't sure he'd go in, Jim. Holy Year or not, it was still touch 'n' go.

He'd parked his motor this time 'n' got out, at least. Best part of an hour ago, when the spire o St Pete's had come into view, he'd swerved into a side street, driven round the block, 'n' headed back in the direction he'd come from. He'd no looked in on his mother 'n' father, no even to see how his da was. He'd no back-tracked to the motorway either but. Instead, he'd come here: the church he'd went to in his last years o primary; first o secondary. God knows what had made him.

The doors were heavy as fuck still. He'd to strain to prise one open. Even in the half-dark, the poster – its jazziness – leapt off the wall.

Stars

in your

Eyes

He had to laugh! 'Thenight, Matthew, ah wannae be – Mark, Luke & John!' Changed days, if that was how they were fundraisin! No much else had changed but, it seemed. Priests were hearin still at tea-time on Saturdays, for one thing. Some poor bastard had left Parkhead early; or hadn't got to go, in the first place.

He made his way to the centre aisle, past the Holy Water. The usual grotty sponge was there; bits bitten out, looked like. He stopped, once facing the altar. He was aware o the choir-loft over his head, no that anyone could see him. That was the last thing he wanted. Being seen or, worse still, *recognised*, would put pressure on him to *go*.

Down here, a handful o others, only, were in. Was alright but: they'd no cottoned on he was there. Two at the front were women. They'd that quiet, intense look about them: the beads; the missal; lips goin twenty-to-the-dozen. One had an old-fashioned fringe. ('A fringe fair snookers ye for wearin a hat', his gran, God rest her, always said.) Their handbags were beside them on the pew, an open invitation to druggies. Time was, women like that would've worn a *mantilla*. Course, when his da dragged him here as a boy, it would've been folk's *grannies* he normally seen. Now, it was likelier to be someone he knew's *mum*. No that he was expectin to recognise anyone. Too long away, they were. '75, his folks had moved –

Flitted.

Snap oot ay it, will ye?!

He snapped out of it –

Still standin there just, he was. How long he'd been stood there for, God only knew. His head was sort-of lowered. If he was honest, he was surprised by the amount o respect he was showin. Even if, these days, he couldn't be arsed wi any o this, he was still showin respect.

He took a good look round. Tried to take things in, discreetly. He was recognisin things. Being reminded o things. Amazed certain things were still there. Paddy Boy, for example, was chasin away snakes still – in the middle window on the left; *St Margaret of Scotland*, on the window-sill opposite. Same rotten old radiators were there 'n' all. Were still thon grotty beige colour. The altar-rail, on the other hand, was gone. As was the wood linkin the side-altars to the main one. Was like they'd got *Changing Rooms* in, or summit. Altar was lighter, brighter.

He decided to risk a nosey; to check out the names above the confessionals. They meant nuthin to him, of course. Old parish priest frae back then, whoever seen him, would be dead now. His juniors, parish priests elsewhere. Been given their own first parish, they would've, then moved on to bigger ones. They could be monsignors, or bishops. *Cardinals*, forchrissake! Could be married wi weans, too, of course. Ye never knew these days.

Once he was done lookin, he sat down. Stepped into the pew without genuflecting. He was buggered if he was goney do that. He didn't kneel, either. Sat there just, lookin; thinkin.

The hymn-book, he lifted automatically. He put it straight back down but. Didnt want remindin. Seein it written down had shocked him once before – the stuff he used to sing, wi'out thinkin. Was time, anyhow, to decide would he *go*. Truth was: he was strugglin. Even if the idea appealed to him sort-of – the idea o forgiveness; forgiveness for all he'd done in the last twenty-five years – the thought o kneelin down 'n' waitin didn't, waitin for the grid to go back.

He sat for a good while afore he slid onto the kneeler. He knew himself from all they years ago: if he carried on sittin, he'd spend the whole time watchin just; watchin all they other cunts. There was something about kneelin down but; bout restin your head on your joined hands. It made ye go still; all holy. Ye started to contemplate, to focus more –

Examine your conscience –

that's what they'd been telt, in P.3, preparin for their first confession. Preparation for a good confession was what Mulvey went on about 'n' all when later visitin their secondary. 'Good preparation is almost as important as the confession itself, boys,' he'd say, the boys from the seminary mouthing the words along with him.

Lourdes, thon time! Same one had run into his gran in Lourdes, sure, Jim suddenly minded. Wee Mrs O'Kane had gone from Letterkenny, Mulvey'd accompanied a pilgrimage from Paisley, 'n' they'd talked to each other wi'out your man realisin he taught the woman's grandson. Jim had spotted him in his gran's photies, visitin the following summer. The day they'd met, she told him, Father'd spent the entire morning wi one of their group. 'Ye want to have smelt the smell o' death off the poor soul'. His gran had sat there, mindin. Then: 'He was a lovely man, Seamus. Is he a good teacher?' she'd asked out of the blue, just as it had dawned on Jim she'd *scrimped 'n' saved* whereas Mulvey was probably *paid for.* He'd found himself tryin to gi'e the bugger credit. Mulvey, after all, had read them *Catcher in the Rye*, even if he censored the 'language'. He tried 'n' all to say confession wasn't a 'burdensome obligation', but a chance to 'repair' your 'friendship or relationship' wi God. His worksheets were full o stories to try 'n' make it interestin: Franz Jägerstätter resistin the Nazis; Door-Knocker Ned; he'd even managed to smuggle Kamikaze pilots in!

That was then.

Question was: the fuck was he doing here now?

Image of him hammerin his left-hand drive came back to him:

> roof down, blazin sunshine
>
> radio on; him gi'in it laldy
>
> the fast road to Playa Blanca.

Signal had cut out just after Yaiza. Middle of a news item. He'd heard enough but to know the first year of the new millennium was goney be a Holy Year; the Vatican was encouragin the faithful to come back to confession. All ye had to do to clean your slate was –

He hadnt heard what – wi the signal cuttin out. Seems, though, there was one o these Holy Years every twenty-five 'n' ye could get absolution for the past twenty-five if ye played along. Part of him was sayin: might as well. Other part was thinkin: fuck it. That part – '*Satan talking*' – couldnt see himself bowin to them now.

Other question, anyhow, was: what he was goney confess? Was he goney let on how long it had been? Did he know even? All he could mind was one year goin in, in preparation for Xmas. A student he'd've been at the time. He'd went in in all sincerity 'n' knelt down 'n' announced he wanted to talk to the priest about *conscience*: 'I need to discuss *conscience* with you, Father,' he'd said. Totally genuine, like. Took a bit o doin, it did, 'n' all. And what happens? Your man wrong-foots him! Miserable oul shite wrong-foots him. 'What makes ye think I've time for that?' your man had snapped through the partition. 'Get on with your confession, youngfella!' He was so shocked, Jim, he'd rhymed off the absolute minimum 'n' ignored the rest. 'Peace 'n' Goodwill to you 'n' all!' he'd muttered as he left the box. His 'tree Hail Mary's and a Glory Be' were still waitin to be said even now.

Beginnin o the end, that was, if he was honest.

He was being stupid – sittin here, no doin nothin. He should be tryin to sort stuff out. In his own head, at least.

Thing was: no goin to Mass, losin his religion, were the biggies 'n' yet there was no point, it felt like, in raisin them. Didnt feel lik he'd *lost* fuck all. Was a case o: the religion he was born into no comin into it any more just. That was the problem: how was he goney say that? What chance was there of *reconcili-bloody-ation* (as they now called it), if that was his openin gambit?

He could always try discussin *sin*, he supposed. Quote the smart-arse who'd pointed out that *sin*, in some languages, means *to be*. So what was wrong wi *being*, like? Good question, that; bloody good question! Lot o the sexual stuff, if ye thought about it, was just about *being*. Way you were. Way you were made to be. What was their problem wi that?

No, he was damned if he was goney tell them sexual stuff. Boy in the box was onto plums if it was stories lik that he was wantin. Jim could just see Pauline's face if he did say owt. Sheila 'n' all: she'd have his bloody balls off. No, he wasnt about to take the beauty out of it by kneelin down in front of some supposed celibate 'n' –

Priest was bound to raise it, if he didnt. Would *hear* he was a grown man. He knew frae Andrew Harper thon time, Jim, that round about the mid 80s they'd started challengin folk; didn't just accept whatever ye rhymed off afore *For these, and all my other sins, I am very sorry*. Handy wee phrase, that. *I told lies* was the other classic. He'd always squeezed it in. Specially if he'd lied through his teeth about how long it was.

O Flower of –

Shit! His mobile!

He fished for it,

fought and died f –

seen it was his mum or dad callin,

and glen

managed to switch it off.

Was alright: looked like folk hadn't noticed. Too deep in prayer, looked like.

Bugger it: he was gettin nowhere; nowhere at all wi this.

A second woman comin out o the only box confessions were being heard in made him realise it wouldnt be long afore it was his turn. *If* he actually went, that was.

He was doin it again: checkin out others, stead o lookin at himself. Thing was: lookin at the one auld boy still to go 'n' the two auld dears who'd been, he couldn't imagine them doin nuthin. What had folk like that to confess? He couldn't see it. The *poverty* of their lives, on the other hand, was written all o'er them. So much so, he felt an old anger returnin. They could be their own worst enemy sometimes, Catholics. Bloody experts, they were, at gettin in their own way –

One more, then it's you, he minded himself.

Thing was: if he didn't react when his turn came, someone was bound to come up to him. He made a mental note to get his arse out o here afore that. No harm to them; they could get to fuck but, if they started wi any assumptions. He looked at his watch. There was a chance, he supposed, the priest would want back for *Blind Date*. *Blind Date* and/or the *Lottery*.

It was time to break out o his dwam. To think this through. To forget all he'd ever learned about 'firm purpose of amendment'. That was how to tackle this:

What did *he* –

Gettin rid o girlfriends in the past cos they were non-Catholics 'n' he didnt want to upset the family, he regretted that. Rest o them – the younger ones – had just got on wi it just. Few years down the line 'n' they were livin thegether 'n' nae cunt blinked –

The look, the hurt, on Morag's face, especially, when he split wi her.

Kids he'd no had was another regret.

Shaggin on the QT. He regretted *now* no being open about it.

Plus, the way he put up wi things. Accepted being powerless when he wisni.

Aye, bloody puttin up wi things.

At work, too. Puttin up wi things at work.

Maybe he was being too hard on himself. Those were all things he'd tackle differently now but; would want to do differently now.

Gettin rid o *Seamus* was another.

The boy who'd come over from Ireland wasn't called Jim. The

boy who'd landed in Scotland was christened Seamus. *Seamus O*'Kane. Switching to plain *Jim Kane* meant an easier life maybe. It also meant folk didn't know but. Who he was. What his background was. He'd insist, these days, on more respect.

He'd leave Tess sooner, too. Release them both sooner from –

Devious – he'd avoid being devious –

And he wouldn't wait for nieces 'n' nephews 'n' a big fuckin emergency afore diggin in to support the family, either.

He looked up. Nothin else was occurrin to him –

The string o stuff had surprised him.

There was somethin calmin about admittin it but; bout lettin it come to mind.

He settled again, to continue. Other thing to sort out was what he wasnt confessin.

Touchin. Touchin 'n' being touched.

Any exchange of tenderness, gentleness. He wasnt confessin that.

No fuckin way.

His books. He wouldn't be apologisin for the books he'd read. For startin to think for himself.

Tellin yir man to get to fuck when he done what he done was ruled out 'n' all. As was his hatred of Thatcher 'n' therefore Blair.

These days, nuthin could snooker him like that did:

What he'd grown up wi –

What had happened to the values he'd grown up wi.

Tap –

He was being tapped on the shoulder.

'That's Father ready for you!'

Jim looked up, his eyes strugglin to focus on the auld guy he'd noticed before. Boy's teeth were horrendous.

'I'm not interrupting you or anything but that's Father ready for you!' the auld yin repeated, gently. 'Poor man's got to get home at some point, too.'

'Okay. Thanks. Thanks for lettin me know,' Jim said.

'I wouldn't disturb you – it's just Father does a wild lot as it is. And he was up these last two nights with old Mrs McInally, God rest her.'

Still in a daze, Jim nodded. The auld guy continued down the aisle.

As for Jim: the decision he'd to make was now starin at him.

He looked in the direction of the confessional, levered himself up, steeled himself, walked along 'n' across 'n' stepped in. Closing the door behind him, he knelt down.

As his knees came down on the kneeler, he finally spotted the grid. The wee door going back helped. He was lookin not at a forehead, but an ear and hair.

'Bless me, Father,' he gave it, having decided to at least say that. To accept the traditional wording, to get things started.

'Bless me, Father,' he began again 'n' stopped.

'It's been – '

He stopped again. Feelings o panic – the instant tearfulness he'd hated as a boy – were ambushin him.

Fucksake: he sounded like he was blubberin.

'God will help you, son,' he heard the priest say. 'Ask him, and God will help – '

Silencio.

Priest was givin him time to ask. When he still didn't continue, Jim, he heard the priest prayin – as if *he* was askin for him.

'Take your time, child'.

That *child* went through him.

All he could think of was the *hold* they'd had. Would still have, if they could. Plus, what your man was supposed to have said recently: bout them being an autonomous organisation, account-able to nae cunt.

Something inside him erupted.

'It's no use. I can't do this, Father!' he announced 'n' got to his feet.

Even callin him 'Father' was a compromise.

'Pray to the Lord for support, child. Think of the Prodigal Son, that beautiful parable. The Good Lord's delight in welcoming you back – '

More silence. Jim visualisin – *able* to visualise, suddenly – the type o confession they *should* introduce. If he had his way, the bloody *priests* would be carpeted: hauled up 'n' made to confess to a whole congregation, each 'n' every one o who would be more lapsed, than not.

'Kneel down again, child. Try and kneel down. To put your pride aside.'

'Naw, mate. Ahm oot o here!'

It had exploded out o him afore he knew it. He couldn't handle this.

Something in him relented. No need to be rude. 'The front gate, mate. If ye want to hear what I've got to say, I'm at the gate. Wee cafe across the road, if ye prefer. It's got to be out in the open but. Or not at all.'

There was an almighty clatter as he left the confessional 'n' made for the exit. He was aware as he went of the priest's door clickin, and of quieter, less urgent steps behind him.

He was damned if he was goney look round but.

Was a toss-up anyhow as to whether or not they were followin.

20

March 1980

The bus reached the brow of the hill. Like every other night, Liam stood up, moved forward, danced off before it stopped; then crossed the road to the 59 Steps; stood and contemplated them. He was no athlete and the speed mightn't be great; he'd do them in a oner but, two-at-a-time. He knew what the deal was, sure, if he failed: it was straight back down to the bottom again. A freezin cold bath if he cracked a second time.

He stood there, psyching himself up, the hold-all wi his books over his shoulder; then something like a pistol went off inside him and he belted off up them.

Practice made the first half a doddle these days. Could even feel good. The third quarter was when he had to dig in; the final flight where he always crumbled nearly, his thighs on the verge of explodin. If he fought through that, he could stumble up the last o them. No one said it had to be elegant.

Tonight, he'd just reached the final flight when his emergency brake kicked in – he'd spotted the numberplate, the Northern Irish numberplate, outside their door.

Something inside him went queasy.

He thought about calling from a phone-box. Making out he'd an essay to finish. Then he remembered the Watt fight but, and forced himself.

'That'll be Young Liam now,' his mum said as he tried to sneak in.

222

His heart sank. He didn't even get time to get his coat off. Door was open and Eugene out on top of him before he'd put his bag down even.

'Wha' about ye, nephew? Ye rightly?'

'Aw, hi!' he said, pretending to be surprised. 'You made it after all? I'm fine, thanks!' he heard himself claiming as they shook hands. 'Yourself?'

The problem wasn't so much Eugene, their da's wee brother. He loved the guy to bits, sure. It was the thought of the others he'd have with him. Derry ones. *Strangers*.

'Mere in tay I introduce ye to me mates!' Eugene said, putting an arm round him. 'Your cousin Owen's over an' all.'

'Are ye lookin forward to the Watt fight?' he asked, to buy time.

'The *Nash* fight, ye mean, kiddo!' Eugene said. 'God, aye! Been lookin forward to it for weeks!'

They couldn't get in for the dog.

'Down, boy! Calm down, boy!' Liam said, hunkering down to pat him. Even from the hall, he could see the livingroom was mobbed. Ciara and Orla were on the rug in front of the fire. Sean, he could see, had his back against the fireplace.

'Full house tonight!' a Derry accent laughed.

Boy wasn't kidding, whoever it was.

'Standin room only!' another voice declared.

It was typical Derry ones. Taking over wherever they went. Always something to say about everything.

There wasn't even standing room. He'd be doing well, it looked like, to pick his way through on tiptoe. Younger ones had planted themselves wherever there was space, determined no to miss anything. Not a single one was out. Wasn't surprising, if ye thought about it. Part from Granda Cluskey or Mammy Donnell coming over for a First Communion or Confirmation, say – this was the only visit they'd had from Derry, ever.

He stopped patting the dog. Spotted the shamrocks and Paddy's Day cards on the mantlepiece. His gran must've sent them. There was a new record playing an' all: *The Town I Loved So Well*; a version he didn't know. It was a different man singing and he didn't like the voice.

His mum looked out of the kitchen. 'Wha' happened ye didn't phone?'

Liam shrugged. Didn't know himself.

Dog was now on its back, demanding a rub. His sisters were watching, laughing. 'If ye think that's bad, ye should see him when he gets excited!' Ciara said to the posh seats behind the door. Liam was catching his first snatches of their terrorist accents: their wee short tight-as-shite vowels. Eugene – the uncle they didn't have to call 'Uncle' – didn't; the others sounded hard as nails but. Ye half expected them to pull a gun on ye.

He inched into the room. There was no sign of his da. 'Hi!' he nodded when he saw his cousin.

'Yes, Liam!' Owen said and came over to shake his hand. Orla was about to grab his seat when he turned to go back. He saw her and offered her his knee. Wee love was cuddling into him even as he lifted her.

'This is my nephew, Liam,' Eugene was now saying. 'First university man in the family – '

Boys on the settee were putting down their ashtrays and mugs of tea to stand up and shake his hand. All about Eugene's age, they were. Two of them still had their coats on.

'Yes, Liam!' the first one said. 'Pleased to meet ye, son.' His fag flicked to his left hand, and he wiped his right on his trousers before he offered it. Was Shamey Rooney, the keeper in their D&D League team. Liam recognised him, now he looked at him, from photos in the *Journal*.

'And this is my best mucker, Colum Reilly,' Eugene continued.

Colum shook hands, then stepped aside to reveal the last of them.

'And that there's Dessie Hume,' Eugene said.

'Last, not least but,' Dessie joked as they shook.

'You the left back?' Liam asked.

Colum Reilly laughed. 'Aye, left back in the dressing-room, maybe, son.'

'Naw, that's *Mickey* Hume you're thinking o', Liam,' Eugene said.

They sat down again, watching not to knock their mugs over. Fairly polished off the biscuits, they had. Liam watched them snatch another puff, then picked his way past Ciara, Cahal, and the dog to get to the kitchen.

'Out of the way, you!' Annette complained as he passed the TV. She kicked him, the wee bitch.

'Your dinner's ready!' his Mum called as they glared at each other.

'Great, thanks!' he said, still staring Annette out.

'D'ye want it in the livingroom?'

'Naw, I'll eat it here.'

He squeezed in against the wall, beside the fridge. His mum looked at him: he never sat in there. Then, just as he was getting comfortable, his da's head came round the door – he must've been in the toilet. He looked fizzin, even before he opened his mouth.

'What are ye doin out here?' he asked. 'Your uncle Eugene's come all the way over to see ye. Don't be so buckin ignorant!'

Liam bit his tongue. 'It's Watt against Nash he's over to see, no me!' he was thinking, when Eugene piped up behind his da: 'Naw, leave the youngfella alone, big brother. Jist leave him alone! It's okay, sure!'

'What's wrong wi' ye?' his mum asked.

'Nuthin.'

She nodded at the mush he was mincing with his fork. 'Least show it some respect, if you're no goin to finish it!'

He put his fork down. 'Weans in Africa, Mum, eh?'

She smiled at him. They both still minded the day, in Primary One, when he'd told her to put his dinner in an envelope and post it to the Black Babies.

She reached across; clasped and shook his wrist.

'Away in!' she said. 'If only to keep your daddy quiet, sure. I thought you liked Eugene?' she added.

'It's no that,' he said.

It was also Celtic buying Frank McGarvey from Liverpool.

'So how long's that you're over here now, Liam?' Colum Reilly was asking when, finally, he took himself back in.

'Ten years, come the summer,' his da said.

'Ten years! Long as that?' Eugene said. 'I was guessing seven or eight, in the car.'

Liam was squeezing in between his sisters. Wee Orla put her arm round him. Sean caught his eye as if to say 'Awright, bruv?' His back was still against the fireplace. He looked comfortable, his body language confident – despite being younger.

Liam checked out the rest of the weans. Like a theatre audience on the floor, they were: no missing a word was said; no saying nothing themselves.

'D'ye miss Derry, Liam?' Shamey Rooney asked.

'Aye, ye always miss it, sure,' their da answered. 'Ye never ever get over the homesickness.'

'Would ye go back but?' Dessie, the stickler for detail, asked.

'Aw, aye! I'd go back tomorrow,' his da said. 'Bridget wouldn't but – '

Liam could see Eugene was listening closely. Was as if his mates were asking the questions The Family in Derry wanted answered.

'I've got the weans to think of an' all – ' his da continued.

Maybe Eugene'd put them up to it, it occurred to Liam.

'I can't understand ye missin Derry, Liam,' Owen said.

'*Uncle* Liam to you – '

Liam laughed to himself. Nice one, Da! Owen'd walked into that one.

'Uncle Liam,' Owen repeated. He wasn't pleased but. 'I'd be away lik a shot!' he bragged.

'And I suppose ye call yourself a Derryman?' their da said, looking at him.

Owen didn't respond, didn't hardly shrug.

'Aye, well I hope ye never have to go, Owen. It'll be a different song ye'll be singin, if ye do – '

'D'ye no lik Scotland, lik, Liam?' Dessie asked.

'Ye jokin? Ye couldn't lik this place!'

'Do the weans lik it?'

'Ask them yourself. Different for them, I suppose.'

'Scotch tongues they've got in their heads, anyway,' Colum said. 'Fairly lost their brogues, they have.'

Best mucker or no, Eugene glared at him: he knew the weans' accents were a sore point with his brother; a very sore point.

Shamey must've spotted the glare. 'Wasn't there not something last year about the Scots getting their independence?' he asked, to change the subject.

Eugene looked relieved. 'Aye, right enough: wasn't there a referendum?'

Their da nodded. 'Buggers chickened out of it but – '

'Wha'? Did they vote against it?'

Dessie sounded like he couldn't bloody believe it.

'Naw, they didn't vote *for* it. Not in enough numbers, anyway. Liam there'll tell ye – '

They all looked over to where he was sitting: against the bookcase. He put down the new record sleeve he was checking out.

'33% for. 31 against. Rest stayed at home,' he said.

'Wha'? And did the mother of all democracies overrule that simple majority?' Colum asked. He either'd his tongue in his cheek or it was a gumboil.

'The then Labour government had introduced a 40% hurdle at the last minute – ' Liam explained. His voice tailed off when he saw they weren't interested.

His da humphed. 'Would ye listen to him!' he said, turning to Eugene. '*The then Labour government*,' he quoted. 'Was him there voted Thatcher in – '

'*Wha'? That oul cow?*' Shamey Rooney croaked, cartoon-style.

Derry Ones all laughed.

'Ye can't mention her name wi'out him doing that!' Owen tried to tell their da. Their da didn't take him on but. He was insisting on Eugene looking him in the eye.

'Your nephew's a buckin Tory, wee brother!' he said when, finally, Eugene did.

'I AM NOT!' Liam protested. 'I told ye before: I voted *Liberal* – for the same reason I don't support the Old Firm.'

His da smiled thon quiet wee smile his gran produced an' all when she wasn't impressed.

'I rest my case!' he said.

Eugene soon wiped the smile off his face but. 'Me Ma's convinced *you* voted Thatcher!' he said.

'*Wha'? That oul cow?*' Shamey Rooney croaked again. Everyone except their da laughed this time.

'Did I buckin hell,' their da said. 'Ye can tell her that an' all!'

Eugene laughed. 'I will!' he said. 'I'll leave out the *buckin* but! Ye know what she's like about cursin!' He turned to Liam. 'Did ye vote for *independence*, at least, mucker?'

It sounded like he was trying to get him off the hook.

'Naw,' Liam answered.

Eugene looked devastated.

'I was still too young to vote at that point, sure,' he added, quickly.

'Aw – right,' Eugene said.

Dessie's head was shaking furiously.

'Wha's ailing *you*?' Eugene asked, seeing his mate looking apo-bloody-plectic.

'No friggin fucker would stay at home if there was a refer-buckin-thingmy up in the bloody Creggan!' Dessie exploded.

Eugene laughed. 'Can I quote ye on that?'

'Language, boyo!' Colum warned but. 'Can't be having thon kinda language in front of Bridget and the weans, now!'

'Leave him alone, Colum, son! He's all right, sure!' their da said.

Shamey obviously couldn't believe his ears either.

'A gift of a chance to get rid o the Brits – an' they don't buckin take it!' he groaned.

'Aye, ye wouldn't credit it, would ye?' Colum complained. He sounded bitter. 'There's us having to fight the buggers! There's the boys bombing and blasting the Brits every chance they get – and there's still not a snowball's chance in hell of a United Ireland!'

'And the friggin Scotch get it handed to them on a plate – and *don't take it*!'

Dessie'd his head in his hands, he was that close to tears.

'Aye, well now ye know why I don't like the Scots!' their da said. 'Is it any wonder I don't like living here?'

Shite, Liam thought. He hated it when this kinda argument went his da's way.

'So who's goney win tonight then?' Eugene asked, out of the blue.

You could see it was sheer devilment – to get a bit of craic going.

'Who's goney be the new WBC Lightweight Champion of the World?'

'Jim Watt!' Sean shouted.

' – is the *wrong* answer!' Eugene continued.

Liam grinned at his younger brother. Ye had to hand it to him: Sean'd the courage to say things.

'Do I have another answer?' Eugene inquired. 'No conferring now!'

'Charlie Nash!' Ciara shouted.

The guys on the settee looked amazed to see a weegirl knowing about boxing.

' – is the *cor-rect* answer!' Eugene announced. 'But *why*?'

'Cos he's got a moustache!' Sean shouted.

The Derry Ones, Eugene included, just looked at him.

'Ciara likes boys with moustaches!' Sean explained.

'Aye, like Fraser Buchanan!' wee Orla said, embarrassing her.

'Who's Fraser Buchanan when he's at home?' Eugene asked. 'Doesn't sound lik a Derryman to me!'

'Naw, youngfella three doors along!' their da told him. 'Buckin Prod, into the bargain.' He turned to Ciara: 'I'll Fraser Bu-buckin-chanan ye!'

'Bet he's not as goodlookin as our Charlie!' Colum said.

'*Goodlookin*?' Sean repeated. 'That's no what it says in the paper today!'

'Naw? Wha' does it say, lik?' Colum asked.

'Says he looks like a survivor from the Famine!' Sean laughed.

'That what it says?'

'Aye: quote-unquote!'

'Cheeky buggers! Wha' paper's that in?'

'*Scotsman*!' Liam answered. He'd seen it an' all.

'Wha's a Derryman lik you doin readin the buckin *Scotsman*?' Shamey jeered. 'Ye want to buy yourself a daycent paper!'

'Aye – lik the *Journal*!' Owen laughed.

'Wha' else does the *Scotsman* say?' Eugene asked, soundin worried.

'Says Nash hasn't the fire-power of Watt. That his body shots aren't as good!'

'That's a whole lot o' shite, that there!' Dessie erupted.

'Sure Watt's scarred o' Nash!' Shamey Rooney reminded them.

Ciara and her da looked at each other. Was news to them. You could see it wasn't but to Sean.

'Aye, sure Watt's been dodgin him! He's *feart* tay fight him!' Dessie claimed.

'Has he?' their da asked. 'Is he?' Ye could hear the hope in his voice.

'Aye, everyone knows that, sure! Sure back in '74, even, Watt wouldn't come to Derry to fight him!'

'Didn't know that, now!' their da said.

'Aye, he even relinquished the British title rather than come over!' Colum confirmed.

'Aye, 'magine!' Dessie sneered. 'Oul cowardy-cat was feart tay set foot in Derry!'

'My money's on Nash, anyway!' Owen declared, confidently.

'Aye, mine, too!'

'Mine, too!' the Derry Ones all agreed.

'Have ye heard about the dead man wi' money on?' Eugene asked their da.

'Wha'd'ye mean: dead man?'

'Dead, dead. – He died recently. Before he died but, he made out a will instructing that a thousand pound was to go on Charlie Nash!'

'Aye!' said Shamey Rooney, ' – an' any winnings are tay go straight tay his – wha'd'ye call them there?'

'Dependants!' Eugene said.

'Aye, dependants!' Shamey agreed. 'That's how confident we are in Derry!' he announced. 'Even a buckin corpse has a bet on!'

He stood up, as if untangling a mike. 'The *new* WBC Lightweight Champion of the World,' he declared, in his best Yankee voice, 'is Mis-ter *Char*-lie NASH!!!'

A big cheer went round the room.

'Aye, that'll be shining bright!' Sean said. Only him and Liam weren't joining in.

'They're planning the celebrations already!' Eugene was telling their da. 'There's goney be a big party in front of the Guildhall. Should be good, ye know. He's uniting the two communities. There's even Protestants rooting for him!'

'God, that's great!' their da said. 'Aye, Nash could make it, right enough. Watt's not invincible, ye know!'

Listen to him! Liam thought.

His da was a turncoat. Same one'd been up out of his seat, cheering Watt on against Pitalua and Robert Vasquez.

This was what the problem was. The nub of the matter. What Liam'd expected to explode from the moment he heard the Derry Ones might come over.

It was Make Your Mind Up time. No sitting on the fence:

are you Irish? or are you Scottish?

whose side are ye on?

That was the question.

It had happened before – with the Home Internationals and the World Cup; Eurovision, even. This time but, they weren't on their own. This time, there was Derry ones here to witness it: *to spot the traitors.*

'*You're* very quiet, mucker!' Eugene was suddenly saying. 'Who are *you* rooting for?'

Liam'd to collect his thoughts, quick. He was caught on the hop.

'Nothing against Nash, but Watt's on a roll,' he said. 'He took the title in twelve rounds. Defended it in nine. Nash might no last half that!'

Sean thumped his back in agreement. Youngfella was killing himself. 'Aye, big brother!' he finally managed to say, 'God knows why themmins there booked a hotel. The fight'll be over that quick, they could've made the last sailing!'

Derry Ones didn't look amused – not one bit. Their da looked like he might make Sean apologise. Liam but just grinned at his brother. Bugger it: him and Sean were the Scots in the house. If ever there'd been any doubt, there wasn't after Archie Gemmill put Scotland 3-1 up against the Dutch. Two of them'd tears in their eyes as they hugged and celebrated that one.

'Some Irishmen you're bringing up there, Liam boy, hi!' Shamey Rooney complained to their da.

Was the worst buckin thing the stupid big shite could've said.

Town I Loved So Well was back on again.

The boy singing it sounded right Republican. He was turning it into something it wasn't. It was one of the few, sure, where the words were words; and not just propaganda.

Liam tried to look round without being noticed.

Wasn't often you got so many *men* in, he realised.

Something told him trouble was brewing; *big* trouble.

His mum must've sensed it an' all. Offering to make more tea, she was, though the kettle was still hot from the last time. The atmosphere was laden, gettin. She looked at their da as she handed him his mug. If she was asking him not to start, he ignored her. He nudged Eugene instead.

'Ye should've been in here last Friday night, wee brother!' he said.

Liam's heart sank. He looked at Ciara. They both knew what was coming.

'We'd a *very* interesting discussion in here last Friday,' their da said, 'about *Confession*. Would've interested you, Eugene: you that was in a seminary for three years – '

He was milking it for all it was worth.

'Wha'd'ye think, lads?' he said, appealing to the boys squashed on the settee. 'Ah'd to march ma two eldest up to Confession last Saturday night. Eighteen and nineteen years of age, and I'd to take them by the hand. You'd think they'd be old enough to know now and *go*, wouldn't ye?' he said.

'Ay?' he repeated when nobody said nothing.

'What was wrong, lik, they weren't going?' Eugene asked, to

break the silence. He looked first at Liam, then to Ciara, as if to let them speak for themselves. They didn't dare.

'How long'd they not been?'

The hurt on Eugene's face was obvious; his *fear* for their *souls*.

'How long? A whole year, if you don't mind!' their da just about roared. 'A whole year! And me that brought them up to go once a fortnight!'

The livingroom was the quietest it'd been since Liam'd got home. Annette was even getting to hear her programme – he hoped she was buckin enjoyin it. The visitors had gone all quiet an' all. Looked like they were feart they might be asked something. Liam knew to look at them they were no saints. No way were they all as holy as Eugene. Owen, there, for starters, had had to marry his girlfriend.

The silence was awful. Ciara didn't know where to look. Sean, for once, wasn't smirking. None of the weans were smirking.

Their da cast his eye along the jury of four. Expecting its verdict *now*, he was. Eugene waited a minute, then sighed a pained sigh.

'Naw, kids. That's not good. What in God's name were yous thinkin of, closing yourselves off to the Lord like that?'

Liam felt relieved. They were getting the chance to explain, at least. It *showed* Eugene worked with the youth.

'We'd been making our own private confessions,' Ciara said, hoping to undo some damage.

'Your own private confessions?' Eugene repeated. His mates were studying the carpet.

'Their own private confessions!' their da confirmed. 'That's what I'd to listen to, too.'

'Naw, weans, ye can't do that,' Eugene declared.

It sounded like he accepted they'd been trying to do right. What they were doing was still very, very wrong but.

'The priest needs to give ye absolution, sure. And how are ye goin to know your penance?'

'It just comes into your head!' Ciara said.

'Jist comes into your head!' their da snorted.

There'd been no persuading him – even though they'd both thought that if, say, '3 Hail Mary's & an Our Father' came into your head, then that was the penance God wanted.

'Naw, weans,' Eugene declared again. 'That's not on.'

He turned to Colum. 'You ever heard anything lik that?'

Liam thought he saw Colum Reilly squirm. He shuddered, at least, then, still studying his dirty-white trainers, said, 'Naw. I couldn't say for sure, lik. But I can't say I have – '

'But the priest at school said, Uncle Eugene, didn't he, Liam?'

Liam nodded.

'Said what?' Eugene pressed. 'Don't tell me he authorised private confessions!'

'He said ye don't have to be in a church to talk to God. Said ye could be in a field or a forest – ' Ciara tried to explain.

'Aye, but that's different. That's *prayer*!' Eugene said. 'I could accept that. That's not the same as making your confession up in the bedroom but – '

Liam thought he saw Owen laugh. He could imagine what that bugger got up to in the bedroom.

'But how not, Uncle Eugene?' Ciara asked. 'How do you need the middle-man?'

'She means *why*,' their da said. '*How*'s what they say over here.'

Eugene couldn't see what she was on about but. He sat, shaking his head.

'But my conversations with God were better that way, than through the priest!' Ciara pleaded.

'God forgive ye and pardon ye, weegirl!' their da said.

He nearly lifted his hand to her. One look from Eugene but stopped him.

Ciara didn't flinch: '*And* I was being genuinely repentant – ' she insisted.

Liam could've hugged her, she sounded that sincere; that *holy*. In a way, she was saying all the things they needed to hear.

Eugene didn't respond. He turned to Liam instead.

'*You*'re not saying much for yourself, youngfella!' he said.

'You know me: no got the gift of the gab!' Liam answered.

'Will ye promise me, at least, ye confessed it?'

'Aye, my da told ye, sure. We were up on Saturday night.'

'And wha'd the priest say?'

'That's between me and the priest and God,' he said, firmly.

He knew he had them on that one.

Eugene looked at his da, and his da looked at Eugene – as if egging him on, to press for an answer. Eugene just let a sigh out but and shook his head.

'Naw, we'll need to be going, Liam, sure, to get to the Kelvin Hall,' he said. 'Was only supposed to be a flying visit!'

The others jumped up.

'Is that the time already, Liam? God, aye, we'll need to be going!'

'Thanks for the tea and the bite to eat, Bridget, love!'

Eugene made a point of hugging Liam on the way out. When they were head-to-head on the front step, he whispered: 'Don't you be losing your faith, now, youngfella. The Devil'll be fighting for your soul up at that there university, ye know. I've heard about the books ye have to read! Make sure you fight the good fight now!'

Liam looked him in the eye just.

'Good man!' Eugene said, patting him. 'Good man.'

Sean and Orla were over like a shot.

'Wha'd Eugene say to you? Wha'd he say?'

He wasn't for telling but.

Shamey tooted the horn and the car drove off. They all waved. Their da waved an' all. Was obvious he wanted to go with them but.

Him and Liam didn't take each other on on the way back in.

Aye, they could get staying up to watch the fight, their mum said. She'd make an exception. They'd to be ready for bed first but.

Even as the thing on before *Sportnight Special* was finishing, the younger boys were in their pyjamas and the girls were in their nightdresses and they were huddling round the TV. Their da disappeared to watch it on the wee black & white upstairs. 'The reception's better down here, sure!' their mum said. He wanted to see it in peace but.

He was no sooner up till he was back down. With a minute of Round 1 still to go, Watt went down to a cracker of a right-hook. Sean and Liam'd looked at each other. It was *Disaster for Scotland!* again, like Johnny Rep pulling it back to 3-2 against the Dutch.

'*Char-lie, Char-lie*,' they heard their da singing. '*Char-lie, Char-lie* – '

'The Irishman who thought he was Big Ben!' Liam muttered.

'*Shite!*' Sean groaned.

Their da's head came round the door. He was laughing that much, his teeth nearly fell out.

Turned out there wasn't even a count. Jim didn't stay down.

'Away back upstairs, Da!' Sean laughed. 'It's no over yet! We'll see who's slaggin who later!'

'Watt's in trouble but,' their da tried to maintain. 'His wee wife's away after running out o' the arena. That's how much confidence *she's* got!'

'*Char-lie, Char-lie* – ' he sang as he went.

The next two rounds were hard to watch. Only late in each did Watt respond like the champion he was and take control.

You could see Sean's relief. 'Jim's the more experienced boxer!' he said.

'Aye – an' the heavier puncher,' Liam agreed.

In Round 4, all hell broke loose. The camera'd just picked up on Mary Peters, there to support Charlie, when Nash went down three times. Watt had been stalking him, and once he felt ready, let fly wi a series of left-hooks.

'*Charlie falls for the first time* – ' Sean said as Nash took a count of nine.

The second nine-count followed in no time.

'*Charlie falls for the SECOND time* – ' Sean whooped.

The weans sat glued to the box. Their mum couldn't watch as Nash rose to his feet. He was soon crashed against the ropes again, and went down on one knee.

'JESUS, CHARLIE! Now's not the time for *genuflecting*!' Ciara screamed.

She was nearly on her knees herself, she was so all-over-the-place on her high heels.

Liam and Sean, sensing blood, looked at each other.

Nash got up but couldn't beat the count but.

'*Charlie falls for the THIRD AND LAST time!!!!*' they roared and went mental.

Ciara, God love her, broke down in tears. Their mum'd to comfort her.

'*Who's sorry now?*' Liam sang, laughing, when he saw her.

'Watt only bloody won cos the referee's a MASON!' she roared out of her and fled upstairs.

Sean, meanwhile, was hugging the box: was kissing the screen every time Watt appeared.

'Hi, boy! You'll get yourself electrocuted!' Bridget warned him.

'Naw, see if you can see Eugene & Co in the crowd, crying!' Liam urged.

They looked like mad; couldn't but.

Then it was Harry Carpenter by himself again.

It was absolute *ages* before their da ventured down. He must've been *gasping* for a cuppa. Liam and Sean were all for heading up and giving him a slagging. Their mum wouldn't let them but. 'No, don't!' she said. '*Don't!* I said. He's hurt enough.'

When their da did come down, he tried to put a brave face on.

'Maybe they'll come back out since it's over early!' he said. 'Maybe Eugene at least'll come. Even if it's the middle of the night. He knows he can turn up at my door anytime, sure!'

The Derry Ones didn't show but. Not even Eugene on his own.

'Ye'd've thought the lousy shite would at least've phoned!' their da said the next morning when he looked at his watch and had to accept they'd be on their way to the boat.

Liam didn't comment. Was rushing out; last minute, as usual. 'Bye, all!' he was about to shout when he spotted Ciara – way she was looking at their da.

Sometimes – there was no two ways about it – the way he went on done your head in. Ye couldn't help yourself. At others, ye couldn't help but feel for him. Right now was one of them times – he looked thon way ye wanted to go over and put an arm round him.

Nobody said or did anything but.

They all *knew*, to look at him, but.

an allergic reaction. . . and other stories

acknowledgements

A number of stories in this collection first appeared in various anthologies and magazines: *Across the Water* (Argyll), *New Writing Scotland* (ASLS), *West Coast Magazine* (Glasgow), *Cutting Teeth* (Glasgow), *Southfields* (London), *Edinburgh Review, Chapman* (Edinburgh), *The Eildon Tree* (Scottish Borders), *Ensuite* (Berne) and *The Recorder* (New York). 'upset easy lip' was published on the websites of BBC Radio Scotland and the Scottish Book Trust as part of the *Days like this* project (2008). My grateful thanks to all the editors involved, not least AL Kennedy and James McGonigal who published my first Liam story. Alison and Jim – like Joy Hendry, Joe Murray, Brian Whittingham and Donny O'Rourke – 'ran with me' more than once. Thank you.

These early publications opened up great opportunities: six weeks in Riga as Scottish PEN's first *écrivain sans frontières*; two months in Grez, thanks to the Robert Louis Stevenson Memorial Award. I have also represented the City of Glasgow in both Berne (Scottish Writing Fellow) and Nuremberg (Hermann Kesten Award); and benefited from residencies at Ledig House (New York State), the Monastère de Saorge (France) and Hawthornden Castle (near Edinburgh) – as future books will (also) reflect. To the individuals and organisations behind these awards, my grateful thanks. To be selected each time was greatly encouraging. For friendships then to grow with Joan Lingard, Fiona Graham, David Kinloch, Catherine McInerney, Simon Biggam and Jean-Jacques Boin – a bonus.

A number of stories have already appeared in translation: German, French, Slovene, Latvian, Hungarian and Lithuanian. Two, in Spanish translation, were runners-up in an Argentinian short story competition. Grateful thanks to the editors involved and to the translators: Andrej Skubic, Andreas Jandl, Guzman Huerta, Doerte Eliass, Zsolt Kozma, Laimantas Jonusys, and Marilyne Bertoncini. A special mention must go to Valda Melgalve who translated two of the stories in what were the final weeks of her life. I shall long remember her husband's brilliant reading at the Latvian Academy of Culture in Riga. *Paldies*, Andris.

I have had the privilege of working with, and learning from, fellow writers and translators in Austria (Vienna & Graz); Slovenia (Ljubljana); Latvia (Riga); Ireland (Galway & Sligo); France (Grez-sur-Loing, Barbizon and Saorge); Switzerland (Berne, Solothurn and Zurich); USA (New York and Ghent); Hungary (Budapest and Szigliget); Italy (Turin and Verona); Germany (Nuremberg and Berlin); Montenegro (Podgorica); and Lithuania (Vilnius and Siauliai). These encounters mean a great deal to me – as continued contact and return visits reflect. Thank you, Konstantin Kaiser, Siglinde Bolbecher, Tina Mahkota, Andrej Skubic, Gregor Podlogar, Iztok Osojnik, Stephen Watts, Adam Czernawski, Alexandra Buechler, Marta Dziluma, Ieva Lesinska, Marc Gaber, Martins Zelmenis, Margita Gailitis, Eoin Bourke, Eva Bourke, Christilla Pelle-Douel, Bernadette Plissart, Franco Supino, Pedro Lenz, Martin Zingg, Lorenz Mohler, Fitz Kusz, Helmut Haberkamm, Mauro Faccioni Filho, Lara Vapnyar, Emily Raboteau, Barry Wallenstein, Gioia Guerzoni, Ada Arduini, Magali Nieradka, Gergely Nagy and Paulette Dube.

Thank you, too, to the teachers and pupils, lecturers and students, with whom I have worked closely in Germany, Switzer-land, France and Slovenia. I am grateful to the Habichs, one and all, and Helmut Egger; to Peter Schranz and Renata Supitar; to Gary Massey; and to Les Fioretti for making things possible. All have benefited from teaching materials on the title story – produced by the British Council in Slovenia and available online.

acknowledgements

I have been fortunate to live through a particularly exciting time in Scottish writing and found the authors in question to be especially open and supportive. Again: my grateful thanks. For a fuller tribute, see 'On Writers & Writing I Wouldn't Be Without' on my website. Events at the Book Festival in Edinburgh and the Goethe Institute in Glasgow first allowed me to work with writers from other countries. For all of these Windows on the World (and Ella's at the Traverse in the 90s), I am most grateful.

More windows, more worlds: my thanks to Kathleen Quinn, Malcolm Pender and Gerry McIntyre – so influential in terms of my German and my French, the languages that have so enriched my life. My thanks, too, to John Cardie for the thousands of miles walked over a quarter of a century, both in Scotland and abroad (and for much more besides, mate).

The Writers' Workshop at Paisley Central Library in the early 1980s has had a huge and lasting impact on me. Thanks, Jim and Jeff.

Hellen Matthews was the first person to publish me. She and Gerry McGrath saw most of these stories first. My thanks to both.

Thanks, also, to Stella Rotenberg, a *loyal* friend. For her poems. Her friendship. And always asking about Liam. For her poem, 'We Have': 'We have nothing / but our flesh / – and vulnerability'. And for the lines: 'The inhuman, / how can I find it / in me?' (from 'Auschwitz').

Special thanks, too, to Colum McCann and Barbara Trapido for their generous support of my work. Colum was the first to identify the 'meld'. Barbara, a gem at Ledig.

Almost finally: I am indebted, beyond words, to my family and friends – none of whom, it should go without saying, should be equated with any of the characters in this book.

Last but not least, I wish to thank Derek Rodger of Argyll Publishing – who in these 'has-to-be-a-novel' times was not only prepared to consider short stories, but has been great at getting them out, both accurately and quickly.

Donal McLaughlin
donalmclaughlin.wordpress.com

Other Books from Argyll Publishing

www.argyllpublishing.com